The Treasure of Cathedral Tower

The Bell Tower at the Ruins of Cathedral Panamá Viejo

John Gillgren

ISBN: 978-1-77374-001-0

Typeset by Edge of Water Designs, edgeofwater.com
Cover design by Edge of Water Designs, edgeofwater.com
Skulls & Cutlases created by Simon Child from the Noun Project

Printed in Canada
987654321

Dedication

Cael Wright—grandson number 7 and a
very welcome addition to the family

An Old Jamaican Song

You was a wise one, Morgan
You was a knowing knave
When you was in your cabin
But now you're in your grave!

You was a flyer, Morgan
You was the lad to crowd,
When you was in your flagship
But now you're in your shroud

You was a stayer, Morgan
You was the lad to go
Across the starving Isthmus,
But now you've gone below

Book Five

The Treasure of Cathedral Tower

Captain Henry Morgan
Privateer? Pirate? Murderer?
Rear Admiral? Or a Pirate General?

The previous adventures of the Cali family …
The Treasure of Malaga Cove
The Treasure of Ching Shih
The Treasure of Ocracoke Island
The Treasure of Jean Lafitte

Scientific research and articles
The Transfer of Learning Among Similar Throwing Skills,
International Congress of Health, Physical Education
and Dance. Vol. XXVII, No. 3, Spring, 199

Chapter 1

The pre-dawn sky was dark with heavy clouds that covered the moon and stars like a blanket. Part of the recurrent marine layer that slowly moved onto the California coast from the Pacific Ocean, these clouds provided exactly what the men aboard the 100-foot yacht *Tiberon* wanted: complete darkness. The yacht moved very slowly with no running lights; she was completely dark.

On the bridge of the *Tiberon*, Mr. Chang gave last minute instructions to two men. They were both criminals who preferred their freedom, but the money Mr. Chang had offered them was more than they could ever hope for.

"You two will take this rubber boat into Los Angeles Harbor," Chang said, "where you will see the lighthouse and head directly to the yacht basin. You do remember the layout of the basin, yes?"

"Yes, we do."

"Good. Now, once you enter the basin you will identify the converted PT boat, *Elaine, et al.* Once you locate that boat, you will sink her." Chang leaned forward in the captain's chair to emphasize his words.

"So we are not taking anything, we're just to … blow it up?" asked Georges, a French Canadian explosives expert who had been trained by the Canadian Special Forces. He had been responsible for destroying numerous bank safes throughout Montreal and he was a wanted criminal by the Royal Canadian Mounted Police.

"The family that owns that boat has caused me much trouble and pain. They need to be sent a message. A couple of years ago while on this very yacht, they had the Coast Guard stop us while we were fishing. When they boarded, the Coast Guard found an old crucifix that I had purchased from a Mexican village. They took it and said it had been stolen. Lies, all lies this family has told. I want that boat sunk."

Chang was not telling the truth. He had, in fact, stolen the crucifix from a small Mexican village in Baja California. When the Coast Guard boarded, they had found him fishing with dynamite, which was illegal. The captain and crew were all taken in and the *Tiberon* was seized. However, Chang was able to escape. It was not the first time the Cali family had gotten in his way, and this was not the first time he had attempted to exact revenge.

The navigator on the *Tiberon* announced that they had

reached their desired location.

"Get your equipment loaded up now and be off," Chang told his two criminal hirelings. "The channel opening is only half a mile due east of here. At this hour there should be no boats heading out, and the Coast Guard are asleep. Find that boat, place the charges as we discussed, set the timer for thirty minutes, and get out of there. Do not get caught. Is that perfectly clear?"

Georges nodded. His companion Julius, the man who would be steering the rubber boat, an American and a thief, was a bit more concerned.

"And what do we say if we are caught?" Julius asked.

Chang pointed his index finger at the men. "Don't get caught."

Georges and Julius walked down the stairs that lead to the fantail where their rubber boat was being towed behind the *Tiberon*. On their backs they each carried enough explosive devices to sink a much larger boat. Georges said he wanted to make sure the *Elaine* went down fast.

Dressed in black tennis shoes, camouflaged pants, black hoodie sweatshirts, gloves, and ski caps, the men boarded the rubber boat, released the towrope, and cast off. When the *Tiberon* was safely away, Julius started up the engine and steered the small craft toward the lighthouse at the mouth of the harbor. He calculated that it would take approximately thirty minutes to reach the boat, and then they would stay by the *Elaine* for only about five minutes—just long enough to place the charges on the hull. He figured they would be gone no more than an hour and a half.

Julius had calculated correctly. It took them just under thirty-five minutes to get past the lighthouse and find the yacht basin. The *Elaine, et al* was easy to identify: her wooden hull was distinctly different from the fiberglass boats anchored near it. He cut the engines, and both men picked up oars to paddle the last few feet up to the *Elaine.* Pausing against the wooden hull, they waited to make sure no one was around and that everything was quiet.

Georges set the timers on the detonators for thirty minutes. Since the *Elaine's* hull was wood, he could not use magnets to hold the charges in place; he needed waterproof tape.

"Hold the boat steady, Julius," he said as he reached down to place the first detonator. He stopped and cussed.

"What's the matter?" Julius whispered.

"I cannot reach to bottom of the hull. I need to put the detonator on the bottom of the hull so when it explodes, the boat will go down fast."

"Are you going to get in the water and place it then?"

"No. I will put it as deep as I can. I'll put one here, and we can move up the boat, and I'll place one up there. Then when they detonate, the boat will tip over and sink."

"Well, hurry up, I don't want to be here any longer than necessary."

Georges placed the first charge, and then directed Julius to paddle the boat forward so he could place the second charge. While they were preparing the second charge, a large yacht cruised by going faster than the posted five-mile-per-hour speed limit. The wake of the passing yacht shook the rubber boat and disrupted Georges. Julius couldn't hold the boat still as it rocked back and forth. When it finally quit rocking, Georges began to install the second charge.

Suddenly, a large plume of smoke and fire exploded from the rear of the boat. Both men were knocked down. Julius screamed and desperately covered his face as the heat from the blast washed over him. Georges tried to yell for Julius to get them out of here, but he never got the words out. The second detonator he was holding went off inside the rubber boat. In a flash the boat was gone, along with the two men.

Aboard the *Tiberon*, Mr. Chang had been looking at the yacht basin through binoculars. He saw both explosions and smiled broadly, shaking his head with satisfaction.

"Your man did well," he said to the captain. "He fixed the detonator to explode in two minutes instead of thirty. Now the *Elaine* is gone and so are those two men. Did you search their cabin for the money I paid them?"

The captain nodded yes.

"Good. Let's get out of here before the harbor police and Coast Guard show up. I don't want to be anywhere near here when Mr. Cali finds out his precious boat has been destroyed."

"How will you eliminate Mr. Cali and his wife?"

"Oh, I don't intend to eliminate them. I want his son and his girlfriend. They have caused me far more problems than the father. I have my plan, and it will be executed very soon."

Chapter 2

Carmine "Snail" Cali and his girlfriend Teri Silva donned their diving gear and slipped into the water for a dive off Malaga Cove, a quaint diving spot nestled between Redondo Beach and the exclusive Palos Verdes Peninsula in Southern California. They had only one afternoon class today at the University of California at Los Angeles, UCLA, so they had decided to make an early dive.

They had been studying the biodiversity of sea life off the Pacific coast of California, and had become interested in the disease that was mysteriously causing the California abalone to die. After only a few minutes underwater, they came across two species of abalone, one red and one green, which showed signs of the disease. They carefully removed them from their rock enclave so they could take them back to the lab at UCLA for further examination.

It was a calm day, and they enjoyed an easy, uneventful dive through Malaga Cove. But during their leisurely swim back to shore, a large barracuda came up and brushed by Teri, so close its smooth skin rubbed against her arm. She tensed, slowing to watch the huge fish as it circled around, mouth opening. Snail moved closer to Teri and drew his knife. Barracudas were far more dangerous and unpredictable than sharks; they were known to attack without any warning or provocation.

Snail pulled Teri back, and readied his knife as the barracuda closed in. But at the last moment it veered away. Maybe it recognized it was about to become dinner and decided against going after its intended prey. They watched as it swam into the kelp bed, the sort of undersea hideout where barracudas were known to hide, and wait for the next meal to swim by. Without wasting any time, the two young divers headed back to shore.

Sitting on the rocks overlooking Malaga Cove, Snail thought back to his previous dive at this spot a few years ago when he and his family found the skull of Thomas Doughty along with a hundred gold ingots and the dinghy that had brought Doughty to Malaga Cove. Thomas Doughty had been a member of Sir Francis Drake's crew on his voyage to discover the fabled shortcut to Asia. Snail also remembered the sudden Pacific storm and how his father Carmine had been injured on the dive.

He felt a sudden twinge of sadness.

Teri noticed while she was pulling her gear off. "What's the matter, Snail?"

"I was just thinking about the last time I was diving out

here. We made that dive from the *Elaine, et al.* Dad spent so much time fixing that boat up—I can't believe it got blown up. I wonder who did it? And why would they? Dad didn't do anything to warrant such an attack."

"I wonder if it was someone that wanted to do us, the family, harm?"

"Like?"

"Chang."

Snail frowned. He had first met Teri a few years ago, shortly after the discovery of Doughty's bones. Her alleged uncle, Mr. Chang, had asked the family to make a dive in Hawaii for the lost treasure of Ching Shih, his great grandmother. They did the dive, but it was a horrific experience filled with constant lies and threats. The family had been held captive by Mr. Chang aboard the yacht *The Golden Hai*. During a storm Snail made a daring escape, made it to shore to get help and was found by Teri. Since that moment, they had become fast friends.

"Ah, it can't be Chang. He's long gone; the Bokor's panther took care of him."

"Are you sure?"

Snail sighed. Not long ago, in Louisiana, Mr. Chang had once again tried to disrupt their lives. But fortunately for the Cali family, a Voodoo practitioner, the Bokor Bernadette Boisson, came to their rescue, accompanied by her black panther. The last anyone saw of Chang was his backside as he ran like a mad man through the bayou jungle screaming in fear for his life with the panther hot on his trail.

"I hope that evil Chang is gone forever," Teri said in a

hopeful tone. He once claimed to be her uncle; but like nearly everything else he said, it was a lie.

He looked at his watch. "It's nearly nine; we should get cleaned up and head back to school. We have the meeting with the counselor at one, and I'd like to grab some lunch before we go see him. You ready?"

"Sounds good," she said. They gathered their equipment, making sure to leave nothing behind, and headed up the long trail to their car.

Teri could tell that something wasn't quite right with Snail today. He had been acting a bit out of sorts all morning, but when she had asked him what was the matter, he responded by saying it was nothing.

They were a happy couple, even on days like today, and they went everywhere together. He supported her in her academic quest to become a forensic pathologist, and she in turn supported his desire to play football at UCLA and to become a teacher. So far they both had been successful in pursuing their quests.

They were both looking forward to their upcoming international study course in Panama, the small country located on the isthmus that connects Central and South America. It was a great chance to learn about the isthmus, the building of the Panama Canal, and all the political and ecological challenges that Panama faced on a daily basis. And they looked forward to making a couple of dives in a country they had never been to before.

Two hours later they were sitting at Rudio's, one of the student union dining eateries located at the Terrace Food Court. As usual Snail had one of his favorite meals, fish tacos and iced tea, while Teri enjoyed her Asian salad with strips of grilled chicken and a diet coke.

As they dined they watched the overhead TV carrying an ESPN broadcast on the past college football season. The announcer was reviewing the season standouts by position. They anxiously waited as the reporter went through nearly all the offensive skill positions before he finally announced the receivers.

The commentator said, "Here's a young man whose name sounds like he should be part of one of the mafia families in New York. His name is Carmine Cali, and I think I'll call him 'hit man' as this kid can hit and run, and run and catch, and then hit and then find someone else to hit. And did I say he could catch?"

Teri smiled at Snail, gripping his hand tightly. He grinned back.

"Watch this footage of Cali colliding with Southern Cal's Beasley Carmichael in this year's game. Yes, that's Carmichael's helmet flying into the first row of seats."

Snail winced on seeing the footage, rubbing his neck in remembered impact from the tackle.

"Cali and UCLA quarterback Washington have established

a great rapport and have been very productive over the past season. Cali is a kid to watch, as he has excellent speed and good size, although he is a bit on the short side of six feet. Even though he's not that big, he plays big. Short, compact, powerful, and he's not afraid to sacrifice himself to get that extra yard."

"Oh, Snail," Teri said, "I am so proud of you, and I know you'll make it to the NFL." She glanced at her watch. "Come on, let's go talk with the counselor. I'm excited about the Panama trip. This will be our first foreign country together."

As they were leaving Rudio's, Snail said, "He is wrong about one thing."

"Oh, what's that?"

"I am six feet tall. Nothing more, but I am six feet."

Chapter 3

The meeting with the counselor took almost two hours. The kids had already selected their classes for the upcoming fall semester and wanted to discuss the Panamanian ecology course with the guidance counselor. The counselor explained that the course in Panama would be intense, as it would go into great detail about the Panamanian ecosystem, endangered species, Panama Canal, culture, the Spanish heritage in Panama and the geopolitical situation in the country.

What Snail and Teri remembered most, however, was a side comment the counsellor made.

"Did you know that the infamous pirate Sir Henry Morgan assaulted Panama not once but a couple of times during the 1670s?" The counselor shook his head. "Morgan, it seems, was a beast. The term 'cruel' would have been a compliment."

Snail and Teri exchanged looks. Snail raised an eyebrow, intrigued.

"Your student group will travel to Panama with Professor Diego Garcia," the counselor continued. "He is a graduate of UCLA and a well-known authority on Panama's history and culture. He is a top-notch person—nothing like Sir Henry Morgan."

As they left the office, heading for the course scheduler, they continued to discuss Morgan.

"I wonder if Morgan was as bad as the counselor said?" Teri asked.

"I don't know, but I'm sure Dad has a book or two about him. We can look him up when we get home. If he has nothing, then in a few weeks we'll find out first hand."

The guidance counselor provided Snail and Teri the necessary documents for early registration. Then the registrar directed them to Du-Juan Systeem, who was the course scheduler. They walked from the guidance counselor's office and back out into the large office with cubicles and registering students. Snail found Du-Juan sitting at this desk, playing Solitare on his computer.

Snail didn't like what he saw.

"Are you Du-Juan?" he asked after a moment's hesitation.

"Yes. Did you need to see me?"

"That's correct. Teri and I are scheduled to do the Panamanian ecology course and need to get signed up."

"Have a seat."

Du-Juan was a young man with a dark but clear complexion, with jet-black hair, dark eyes, and a body so slight it might have been made with pick-up sticks.

Teri and Snail sat as instructed, and Du-Juan seemed to notice that their expressions weren't friendly.

"I don't mean to be testy," he said quickly, "it's just that I've had a day that hasn't been very pleasant. I'm sorry, let's start over. Good afternoon, I'm Du-Juan. May I help you?"

He turned out to be helpful, but on occasion asked annoying questions that were not necessarily of importance: why were they taking an ecology course? And together, at that? Had they been a couple long? What interested them in Panama? You play football, what's it like to get hit?

Snail and Teri answered the questions, but with very short answers.

During the conversation they learned that Du-Juan was a second-year student studying business administration and had been offered the position he now filled by an anonymous contact.

"I don't know who it was," he sneered in a way that irritated Snail, "but the university was glad I came along."

Their registration process finally complete, Snail and Teri strolled back toward the dormitories. Teri was looking forward to a quiet afternoon together, and she was surprised when Snail suddenly remembered an important errand he had to do.

"I need an hour or two," he said hurriedly. "I'll meet you at your dorm room, then we can head home for the weekend. Okay?"

"I suppose," Teri said. "What's this errand? You never said you had to do something today."

"It came up at the last minute. It's nothing to worry about. I just need to be fitted for a new lining for my football helmet. That's all. Bye, I'll see you shortly." He kissed her and darted off.

In the registrar's office, Du-Juan Systeem sat in his cubical, thinking of Snail and Teri. They had seemed like a normal, pleasant-enough couple. He wondered what had interested his benefactor in them. Sure, you didn't see many football jocks interested in science and ecology, but people could surprise you.

The Panama thing was new, though. He was lucky he had heard about it so early. He pulled his phone out of his back pocket, and tapped a contact on the list. It rang hollowly twice before he heard a click.

"Hello, Mr. Chang?"

Chapter 4

When the kids returned home to Redondo Beach, Snail's parents Carmine and Elaine were busy preparing for the family reunion the next day. They were anticipating a big crowd and Carmine was busy putting together his famous shrimp, pork, and chicken shish kabobs while Elaine was making desserts.

The twins, Snail's younger siblings Carmen and Caroline, said they would help and asked their mother what she wanted them to do. They playfully pushed at each other, and got in each other's way, throughout the kitchen.

Seeing that they'd only be adding to the crowd in the kitchen, Teri and Snail decided to look up something first. They darted off to the family den, and Snail pulled out one of the books his dad had on pirates. He quickly found Morgan's name and began reading.

"This book says he was an Admiral in the British Navy, plus a pirate general, and privateer. How can he be all at the same time?"

"I have no idea. What does it say about Panama?"

Snail read on, interested on finding out how notorious Morgan really was. "It says here he married his cousin, bought a sugar plantation on Jamaica and raided many countries in South and Central America. It says that he raided Panama twice, and ..." Snail read on then stopped. "What a despicable man!"

"Hmm?" Teri peered around, trying to read over Snail's shoulder. "What does it say?"

He looked at Teri and said, "On his first raid to Panama City, Morgan and his pirates used the local nuns and priests as human shields. When he raided Panama a second time, rather than being captured and used by Morgan again, the priests and nuns ran to the Cathedral Tower in Panamá Viejo, the Old Panama City, said a prayer, joined hands, and then leaped to their deaths. What a tragedy."

Teri looked at Snail with sadness in her eyes and spoke quietly. "Some people just don't have any compassion for the innocent. It's the innocents who are always hurt." She paused a moment then said, "I don't want to know any more about Morgan and what he did. Let's go help your parents."

"Sounds good to me."

Cali family reunions were always exciting. With the money Carmine and Elaine had received for capturing and turning in Mr. Chang in Hawaii, plus a reward for finding the footlocker of gold aboard the Russian tanker Saratov off the coast of North

Carolina near Ocracoke Island, as well as the hidden coins found in Louisiana, the family had purchased a beautiful new home. It was not too far from their previous one in Redondo Beach but large enough to hold all the children, grandchildren, and extended family members.

With their portion of the reward, Snail and Teri had purchased a new car, something more practical for them to use for traveling, diving, surfing, and going out. They sold the old Chevy woody station wagon to an antique car dealer for a handsome price—he made them a deal they couldn't refuse— then wisely invested the rest of their money in a savings account to be used in the future.

Snail and Teri were discussing their upcoming summer course in Panama with the family. Carmine, Elaine, and the twins had already heard, but it was news to Snail's older sister, Maria, her husband, and their grandparents. She held her baby son, Dominic, on her hip while Snail played with his nephew's nose. The only family member not present was Snail's eldest sister Theresa. She had moved out of state and was now living in Colorado with her family.

Also attending the party were 'Tsunami' Tommy and Lani Osawa, the godparents of all the children and dear friends of the Calis.

Teri's cousin Moki Loo Tsing had flown in from Pearl Harbor, Hawaii, to conduct a meeting in Long Beach at the Naval shipyard, so he was also able to attend the reunion. Moki was a senior Naval Criminal Investigative Service (NCIS) Special Agent. He was responsible for the rescue of the Cali family after Mr. Chang had taken them prisoner in Maui. Since that time, he had become a welcome visitor to the Cali household whenever he was in California. The Calis happily referred to Moki as their newest son.

Moki carried with him a letter from Oscar Chin, an elderly gentleman living on Maui who had been a longtime friend of Dr. Silva, Teri's father. In his letter Oscar mentioned he was doing well, and congratulated them on their successes and wished them all good fortune.

The hour was late and the guests were starting to pack up their belongings to head home. But before anyone left, Snail made an announcement.

"Tomorrow Teri and I are off to Panama, but before we go, there is something I want to say."

Everyone stopped and listened as Snail began to speak.

"Well, yesterday I told Teri I had to be fitted for a new helmet lining. She thought that was unusual because I always take her with me. I couldn't do that this time. The fitting wasn't for a new helmet." Getting on one knee, Snail took Teri's hand.

"There is no one I would want to spend the rest of my life with except you." Snail reached into his pocket and withdrew a small dark blue box and opened it up. Inside was a beautiful engagement ring. He removed it and placed it on Teri's ring finger.

He looked up into her eyes. "Teri, I love you so much. Teri Ting Pao Silva, will you marry me?"

There was a long suspenseful pause. Everyone was quiet. Teri looked at Snail.

"Holy guacamole, Snail, I thought you'd never ask. Yes, I will marry you." They embraced and kissed.

The family was overjoyed. Everyone was hugging and smiling until Carmine told everyone one to be quiet. A silence fell over the group as Carmine walked over to Teri.

"Teri, you stole my holy guacamole line. I'm the one who is supposed to say that."

"That's okay. When we get married, you can say it all you want." They all laughed.

Chapter 5

The UCLA student trip to Panama began at Los Angeles International Airport late in the afternoon. The class assembled at the ticket counter, and as a group went through security and passport control, finally settling themselves on the plane. Snail hadn't noticed it before but Du-Juan Systeem was also taking this course. He leaned over and whispered in Teri's ear.

"Did you know that Du-Juan was taking this course?"

"No, he didn't say anything to us when we registered."

Snail gave a big sigh then whispered, "He's one strange dude."

"Snail, that's not nice to say."

"I know, I'm sorry, but it's strange that we never saw him until now. I wonder if he was hiding or something."

Du-Juan sat in the plane right behind Snail and Teri, but he never once engaged in any conversation with them or anyone else. He remained quiet and observant, practically invisible to everyone.

The flight took them first to Mexico City, Mexico, for a brief stopover and refueling. From there they flew to San José, Costa Rica, to pick up a few passengers, then on to Panama City, Panama. There were twenty-two students traveling on this course plus Professor Diego Garcia, the sponsoring professor from the University of Panama.

Professor Garcia was about six feet tall but slightly built. His short hair was dark, with streaks of gray running through the temples, and he sported a mustache that was neatly trimmed. Teri commented that he was quite handsome.

"Bienvenido a Panama," Professor Garcia said, once the entire group was through customs and gathered in the hot evening air outside the airport. "Welcome to Panama. Gather around for just a moment. We are going to take a bus to the university where you will receive your room assignments, and afterward I will pass out itineraries for the time you are here. For dinner, the University will proudly welcome you to our country with a dining experience that is typically Panamanian."

Professor Garcia provided the students with important cultural information on what to do and what not to do in Panama. He answered questions, and then they were ready to depart. They all boarded a bus for the short drive to the university.

Even at this hour the sights and sounds of Panama were amazing. The delicious smell of food cooking over open fires greeted everyone's nostrils. The trip to the university took just

over half an hour, but once there, it was the beauty of the school
that impressed everyone.

Du-Juan was careful to choose a seat directly behind Snail and
Teri. He had been directed by Mr. Chang, the man responsible
for his employment at UCLA, to stay as close to them as
possible. *Learn as much as you can about their habits and plans,*
Chang had said, directing him to report on their every move.
Du-Juan thought that would be easy, just watch what they did
and report. He thought it was odd that Chang would want so
many intimate details on what the kids were doing, but then
if he was writing a book, he would want to know the details of
their daily lives. Little did he know what Chang had in store
for the young lovers.

Chapter 6

The next morning, the students took their seats in an experimental open-air classroom. Professor Garcia took to the front and gestured at their surroundings.

"We at the university are trying an experiment with open air classrooms similar to the ones used in the US. On this wing of the university we have removed all of the walls separating the individual rooms." He stopped speaking briefly and looked around, gave a small grin then continued. "Personally, I don't care for the open air concept because there is no privacy. Each teacher or professor has his or her own agenda and we all teach differently. And if it rains, where do we go?" He smiled around at the visiting students, and surveyed the rows of vacant seats that would be filled when the new semester started up. He shook his head. "But enough of that. Let's get started."

Professor Garcia introduced his staff, made a few jokes, and got some laughs. When everyone had settled back down, he asked the students his first serious question of the day.

"What is an ecosystem?"

"An ecosystem is a community of plants and animals living and interacting with one another, sharing their available resources." Snail answered after a moment's hesitation.

"Very good answer, but there is more. Anyone else what to chime in?"

"An ecosystem encompasses all aspects of the environment, including plants and animals plus air, water, and the sun's energy," Teri offered. "A good example of this is a pond because they host birds, frogs, fish, plants, and microscopic organisms."

"Excellent response. Thank you. Second question: can anyone describe to me the Panamanian ecosystem?"

The students all looked at each other, wondering how to answer.

"The Panamanian ecosystem," Professor Garcia said, "is like any other ecosystem, complete with a large variety of plants and animals. But despite our small size, Panama is home to over 900 species of birds, mammals, amphibians, reptiles, and marine life. We have a large rainforest, or jungle, as some people call it, which should fascinate everyone. There is enough here to keep a student busy for a lifetime."

Professor Garcia looked around at the wide-eyed students and clapped his hands together with a sudden grin. "So let's gather up our supplies, and be off on our first exploration of beautiful Panama."

"This sounds like so much fun," Teri said to Snail, as she unconsciously twisted her new engagement ring around her third finger, "I can't wait to see Panama."

"Me either. Do you have the water, camera, and bug juice?"

"Yes, let's get on the bus."

Excitedly they rushed off and climbed aboard. They were anxious to get started, but had no idea of what awaited them on this journey.

While Teri and Snail headed for the bus, Du-Juan disappeared into a nearby office that was unoccupied. He made a cell phone call that was answered on the second ring.

"We will be traveling through the Panama Canal Zone and then to the Canal itself," he said. "Later today we will be driving around the countryside."

"What is the plan for tomorrow?"

"According to the itinerary we are going to visit Panamá Viejo and the Cathedral of Nuestra Señora de la Ascunción and their famous watch tower. I think the professor is going to talk to us about the pirate Henry Morgan and his raids on the city. We are supposed to be there for some time."

"Good, just continue to report their activities to me."

"Okay."

On the bus, Professor Garcia gave the students a thorough background on the history of Panama and the architecture of the buildings in Panama City. The city was gorgeous; the buildings, churches, and some of the homes were magnificent.

The rest of the morning was spent driving around and viewing from different locations the Panama Canal. They observed the ships entering and leaving various sets of locks. The students were impressed with the engineering that went into the construction of the canal, and were amazed to learn that the locks actually worked on negative gravity. Professor Garcia was a great resource, providing them with the history of the building of the Canal along with some of the hardships that went along with the construction.

For lunch they dined at El Trapiche, on the Via Argentina. Their specialty was Panamanian foods of all sorts, but Professor Garcia had arranged for a typical Panamanian meal for everyone: rotisserie chicken, black beans and rice, salad, and the most incredible flan for desert. Afterward, there was some brief time for the students to wander around the city by themselves.

"Be careful where you eat," Professor Garcia warned them. "Some of the restaurants don't meet American standards for cleanliness, and especially don't drink the water."

As they strolled down one of the beautiful avenues, Snail and Teri admired the many Spanish-style homes, manicured lawns, and expensive cars in the driveways. The kids discussed the façades of buildings and how much they resembled Old Spanish architecture, which was very similar to the building style in Southern California. However, the sights, sounds, and smells they encountered were all new.

That evening when the group was having dinner, one of their class members, Juliana Chamberlin, asked Professor Garcia a startling question.

"Professor Garcia, I have read that there are shrunken heads in Panama. Is that true?"

"Ah, Juliana, that is an interesting question, and to be honest with you it's one we don't like to discuss. But to answer your question, shrunken heads exist in Panama." He made a funny face at the thought of looking at a shrunken head, and the students all laughed at his expression. He reluctantly explained, "According to rumor, the shrunken heads came from warriors who were killed in battle." Garcia gave a sheepish smile and shrugged.

"Professor," Du-Juan asked, "if there are no wars these days and no one is killed, where do the heads come from?"

"I believe the heads are actually counterfeit. In other words, someone might steal a head from the morgue, or they use monkey's heads. Not very ethical, if you ask me, and quite gruesome."

"But where does the whole practice of shrunken heads come from?" Juliana persisted.

Professor Garcia considered for a long moment. "I am from the Darien region of Panama, and my family are members of the Jivaro Indian tribe. They did shrink heads but that was many years ago." He smiled disarmingly. "I think the best thing to remember about a shrunken head is to leave it alone. Don't get caught trying to bring one into the US. If you are caught, it's jail time. Stay clear of anyone selling them."

Professor Garcia looked at the students around the table, quickly changing the subject.

"Everyone done? Good. We are just in time to drive to the Amador Causeway and watch the sunset. The sun sinking into the West is a spectacular sight that must be witnessed at least once on your stay here in our country."

Later that evening, Mr. Chang quietly arrived in Panama. He had already found the perfect men to work with. None of them were too friendly looking, and they were willing to do just about anything for the money that he offered them. The leader of the group was Roberto Vega, a man with a long list of criminal arrests ranging from fighting to theft to disturbing the peace. Assisting Vega was Pedro Lorino and Manuel de Costa. Vega had met them when he was in prison. He liked them and knew they would do the job Chang wanted done.

Chang flipped his hair back away from his face nervously.

"The day after tomorrow, Professor Garcia will have his students diving on an old wreck off the San Blas Islands, and I want you to strike before they leave the city. They are supposed to be at Cathedral Tower tomorrow. I want you to be there and make sure that meddling kid Snail does not get in the way, and I want his girlfriend taken prisoner. Now, here is the money I promised." He tossed two bundles of Panamian balboas on the table. "In two days' time I want her to be here with me, if not before."

"How do we know who the right lady is?"

Chang took out his phone and flipped through the photos. He found what he was looking for and twisted the phone around to show the men on screen. "This is your target. Her hair is longer now, but you should be able to spot her easily."

"How do you know she'll be at Cathedral Tower?"

"I have information from a reliable source, someone who works for me at the university," Chang said. "I know the information he tells me is correct."

While Chang tucked his phone away, he nervously flicked at his hair again, exposing his ears. He still wasn't used to feeling that part of his ear that was missing. Just the thought of it made him feel more determined than ever to make those two troublesome brats pay.

Chapter 7

In the morning, the students boarded the bus for a tour of Cathedral Tower, made famous by the British pirate Sir Henry Morgan. When they were standing in front of the tower, Professor Garcia explained that there were actually two old cathedrals in Panama City.

"This one we will explore today, and the other is Iglesia de San José, or Saint Joseph's Church. Iglesia de San José is the church that actually housed the golden altar Morgan wanted to get his hands on. But when the priests learned that Morgan and his men were quickly advancing across the country, they found a way to hide the altar.

"Legend says they placed the altar aboard the sailing ship *La Santissima Trinidata*. It was supposedly taken out to sea and then hidden on a remote island until the pirates departed."

"What happened to it?" Snail asked. "Do we know what island it was hidden on?"

"Actually," Garcia said with a smile, "it never left the city. The priests hid it in plain sight. They covered the altar with mud to make it look unappealing and left it right here on these cathedral grounds. Morgan never noticed it was standing right over there, partially hidden by the trees.

"But what was even more astounding was the fact that a couple of surviving priests were actually able to convince Morgan to make a donation to the church! After Morgan gave his sizeable donation to the church and left Panama City, priests from neighboring villages came to the city and carefully cleaned and polished their altar before placing it back at the front of the church. Everyone was happy that he had not taken their prize."

"But Professor," Teri asked, "didn't the mud damage the gold?"

"Morgan would have been furious if he had found out, but the altar was actually made of mahogany and only covered in gold leaf. It was only valuable to the people who used the church. It would not have brought Morgan much money."

Professor Garcia looked out across the ruins.

"We unfortunately cannot enter the structure because of its condition, but you are allowed to walk around it, and go up to the opening and take pictures. Just think of the history that this building has seen over the years. It has seen everything from the glory days of Panama to the raids by Morgan to those unfortunate events of today. This church has seen it all."

As the class broke up and went their various ways, Snail

and Teri strolled toward the entrance of the cathedral and looked inside.

"It's a shame all we can see are broken pieces of block and trash," Snail said sadly.

Teri asked, "Just how big was this cathedral?"

"It was a four-story structure with an open balcony at the top," Professor Garcia said, walking up to them. "That is where the Religious gathered together, prayed for forgiveness, joined hands, and jumped. In its day, it was considered a beautiful and majestic building with lavish landscaping around the exterior."

The group wandered around the ruined cathedral, taking pictures, including many selfies, as they enjoyed the sights. A couple of class clowns decided to see if they could enter cathedral but were stopped by the professor before they ventured into the unsteady building.

"That is not a good idea," Garcia admonished them. "Not only are the walls unsafe but snakes have taken up residence in the rubble. If you don't want to be bitten, don't go in."

After a couple of hours at the cathedral, the students were led downtown to have a look at the many splendid churches and other buildings. One attraction that most of the students wanted to see was the churches. They walked up to one of the larger Catholic Churches and were amazed at the stained glass windows.

Snail and Teri strolled along with their roommates, Eamon O'Connell and Christina Barboni.

"The churches here are very different," Eamon exclaimed, "much more ornate than those in Ireland."

Teri was unconsciously playing with her ring again, and Christina asked her about it. She happily retold the story of how she and Snail met, their scuba diving adventures, and concluded with the details of how Snail proposed to her.

They picked up some oranges, chips, and bottled water for the trip to the San Blas islands from an open-air market they came across. There were stacks of fresh fruit and vegetables piled high on carts.

"If the fruit cannot be peeled," Christina said, "then I suggest we buy some Clorox to wash it before we eat it. We don't know where it's been stored or how clean it is."

Everyone thought that was a sensible idea.

To Teri and Snail it appeared that Eamon and Christina were getting along pretty well. Eamon was from Limerick, Ireland, and was a stocky bull of a young man who played soccer. He spoke with a strong Irish accent that was sometimes difficult to understand. He tried to use as much American slang as he could, but it sounded strange with his Irish brogue. Eamon was studying to be physical therapist and had been in a lot of classes with Snail.

Christina came from an Italian and Spanish background and she too was studying to become a physical therapist. She was also the captain of the volleyball team and was easily four inches taller than Eamon. He didn't mind a bit, and was clearly captivated by her shoulder-length, jet-black hair and raven eyes. They made a lovely couple and were becoming near-constant companions to Snail and Teri.

From a short distance away, Vega, Lorino, and de Costa watched the students as they visited various churches of interest.

"Now that the group is split up and many are not paying any attention, I think we can go after the girl," Vega whispered. "It looked like the girl and her boyfriend are walking by themselves. Let's go."

The three criminals charged forward, thinking to just knock over the boy, grab the girl, and keep on running.

The girl spotted them as they ran, pointing quickly to her boyfriend. He took a long look, meeting Vega's eyes fearlessly, and then stepped forward. Lorino was in the lead and he slammed into the kid—and stopped dead as the boy lowered his shoulder in a powerful block. The impact knocked the wind out of Lorino as he fell back, hit the ground, and bounced like a rubber ball.

Vega saw what happened to his partner, quickly pulled up, and stopped. De Costa was beside him and they both looked at Lorino.

"Let's get out of here," Vega said. "We can't have a prolonged fight on a public street."

Both men spun around and took off. Lorino kicked the boyfriend in the thigh with his heel. He staggered back and Lorino was up and running after his friends.

Snail's leg ached from the kick, but he started after the three strangers who had attacked them.

"No, Snail!" Teri called out. "It's not worth going after them."

The three men disappeared quickly. Snail watched for a few seconds before the returned to Teri's side.

"Are you okay?"

"Yes. I am, thank you. Come on, let's catch up with the group."

They met up with Eamon and Christina.

"What was that all about?" Eamon asked.

"I have no idea," Snail said. "Probably some guys thought they could rob us and get some fast cash I guess."

"I'm a little nervous all of a sudden," Christina said, looking around at the street. "Maybe we should rejoin the whole group."

After the students had returned to the university, Professor Garcia came to Snail's room to speak with him and Teri about the thwarted attack.

"Snail, do you have any idea of who those men were and what they wanted? Have you seen them before?"

"No idea. I think they were just a bunch of punks who were out trying to make an easy score on a tourist. Since they didn't get any money and no one was injured, I'd just as soon let the episode go and not worry about it. I don't think they will try anything else with us."

"So you don't want to notify the police?"

"Nope, it's over and whatever they wanted, they didn't get."

"Okay, you're probably right. If we get the police involved, they may hold up our trip to San Blas. We are on a tight schedule and can't afford to be tied down with legal issues." He gave Snail a friendly pat on the shoulder. "I'm glad you're both all right."

Chapter 8

At precisely 6:00 a.m. the next morning, the bus was loaded with sleepy students and began the long drive across the isthmus.

"It is a three-hour drive to Portobelo," Professor Garcia informed them. "There we will stop for lunch, then another short drive to San Blas Point. So get comfortable—we have a long drive."

The trip through the interior of Panama was fascinating, very different from driving around the capital city or the Canal Zone. The jungle came right up to the roadside, shading the street from the sun. Native villagers were often seen walking along the road, with baskets of fruit and vegetables balanced precariously on their heads. On one occasion a woman was carrying a basket of what Snail swore was bugs.

As the hours passed and the students had many chances to

see the native villagers, it became clear that the natives in the region were a mixture of Caucasian, African, and Native Latin American bloodlines.

There were many houses along the jungle road and on the hillsides mostly single-story with thatched roofs. The walls looked like bamboo or sugarcane stalks and many of the floors were simply dirt.

Small kiosks or rickety stands were positioned occasionally along the roadside displaying decorative cloths.

"These artistic pieces of cloth are called molas." Professor Garcia explained. "Molas are a textile art from the Kuna people. They feature complex designs and are constructed with multiple layers of different colored cloth in a reverse appliqué technique. I'll show you." He ordered the bus driver to pull over and stop so the students could get a closer look at the molas.

Christina was familiar with molas from her own childhood. She invited Teri to look with her. The two young women walked up to a small sheltered kiosk that was maybe ten square foot with a long, cluttered table displaying a variety of molas. Some molas were made into blouses, some into dresses, and a large number were designed as tapestries. All were made with bright brilliant colors and designs. Some of the molas displayed turtles, birds, geometric designs, flowers, floral bouquets, pineapples, and even one of baby Jesus with Mary and Joseph.

"These are incredibly beautiful," Christina said as she picked up a blouse to admire. "My problem is that they won't have any that will fit me. I'm soooo much taller than the average Panamanian."

"No problem," Eamon joked, "maybe we could sew two blouses together end to end for you."

That got a chuckle from their friends and a punch on the shoulder from Christina.

Teri mentioned that the prices were so inexpensive that they could buy some for all the family. She started flipping through a stack that could easily be used as a tapestry. She quickly found one that had two fish fashioned in various shades of pinks and blues with geometric designs around them. She also found one that had a large turtle, another with a lobster, and one with a dragon. She selected one each for Elaine, the twins, the Osawas, and Moki. She selected two for her and Snail. She even picked up a couple of handbags with various other mola designs. The woman who waited on them wore a blouse with a large calico cat on the front, and a wrap around her waist that was also in various geometric designs of dark greens and blues.

When Teri was paying for her purchases, a large hairy tarantula slowly made its way across the table. When Christina and Teri saw the spider, they both screamed and jumped away from the table.

The women helping them laughed hysterically at the girls' reaction. She casually picked up the spider, said something in Spanish, and then tossed the spider off to the side.

"This spider," she said in broken English, "she no dangerous."

"How does she know it's a female?" Christina asked as she made her way back to the table.

"Probably because she's an old friend," Teri nervously laughed.

While Teri and Christina recovered from the spider ordeal,

Snail and Eamon ventured over to another stand and examined a display of weapons, mainly spears and knives. On a rack behind the weapons, Snail noticed something that captured his attention. It looked like a shrunken head, or what he imagined a shrunken head to look like.

"Eamon, take a look at this. Is that what I think it is?"

Eamon came over. He studied it for some time before he said he thought it was a fake.

"No fake," said the vendor. "Real."

"Real? Oh man, that's so unreal." Eamon chuckled. "We don't have any of these in Limerick."

Snail and Eamon examined the shrunken head closely. Even though it was offered to them, they didn't touch it. They remembered what Professor Garcia had said. It was creepy looking. In fact, it was much smaller than what either one expected. The skin was wrinkled and dark. Its nose looked normal but tiny. Its mouth and eyes were all sewn shut with some sort of string. And the ears had what looked like earrings of some sort.

"I wouldn't want this to happen to my worst enemy," Snail whispered. "Remember what happened in the movie *Beetlejuice*?"

"I never saw that movie."

"Really? Well, what happened was some creature put a dust on Beetlejuice's head and it shrank. I don't think that happened here."

"I would say not. That must have hurt. Come on," Eamon said, glancing up. "Professor Garcia is calling us back to the bus."

They hurried to catch up with the girls just as they were

getting on the bus.

The minivan was full, carrying Vega, Lorino, de Costa, and a new man, Mario Nuñez. It had been a long ride, too, as they followed the bus of foreign students through the countryside at a discreet distance. The driver came around a corner and had to slam on the brakes as they saw the bus pulled over and the students milling around some roadside stalls.

"Keep going," Vega said to the driver. "Drive another kilometer or so, then pull over and we can wait for the bus there."

The driver did as he was directed. They waited on the side of the road for the bus to pass them. When it did, the four passengers all made sure they were looking away to hide their faces from view.

"Let's go," Vega said, "but not too close."

The bus stopped at an outside eatery in Portobelo, where the chef was grilling chicken and fish. Professor Garcia reminded the students that they would eat here and take a short break before heading on toward San Blas.

Outside the eatery, the students gathered around the professor as he began telling the pirate history of Portobelo.

"Portobelo," he said, "is a small town that was established in 1597 by Spanish explorer Francisco Velarde y Mercado during the Spanish colonial period. There is a legend that Christopher Columbus named this port 'Puerto Bello' meaning 'Beautiful Port.' There is another legend that Sir Francis Drake is buried in a lead coffin somewhere just off the point, but that has never been confirmed."

Snail nudged Teri's shoulder with a grin.

"The man did get around," he whispered.

She rolled her eyes at him, albeit with a loving smile.

"Portobelo has a small population of only about 3,000 residents," Garcia continued, "but it is famous because the Spanish used this port to move silver and gold back to Spain. The harbor is deep so larger ships could come in, load up, and depart without fear of damaging the hull. The ruins of Fort San Lorenzo, which you can see from here," Professor Garcia pointed their gazes to the site, "have been identified as a United Nations UNESCO World Heritage site."

From what the students could tell, the ruins were just that—ruins. Portions of the fort remained but most had been destroyed. The crumbling fort sat on a small peninsula, more of a spit of land surrounded on three sides by the Chagres River.

"The fort sits at the mouth of the Chagres River," Professor Garcia continued, "and this is where Morgan set up his headquarters and base of operations. The Chagres was important to Panama as small boomtowns sprang up, but when the Canal was built, and the Gatun Dam constructed only seven miles from here, the fort and surrounding villages became ghost towns.

"We all know the story of Henry Morgan's raiding Panama twice but did you know that, about sixty years before Morgan came here, a privateer named William Parker attacked and captured Portobelo in 1601? Parker came with a small fleet of five ships and only two hundred sailors and pirates, and captured the city in a daring raid executed in the early morning hours.

"A short but fierce battle took place and many of the Spanish defenders were either killed or captured. In less than twenty-four hours, Parker and his men stole everything they could, loaded up their ships, burned the city of Portobelo to the ground, and departed. The only good thing that Parker did was release the captives taken in the raid."

"Sort of what Jean Lafitte did with the British prisoners he captured when saving New Orleans," Snail said.

"Yes," Professor Garcia replied. "Sounds like you know a thing or two about Caribbean pirates, Snail."

Snail just smiled.

Chapter 9

Within an hour they arrived at the hotel. There were six students who were doing the diving portion of the course and they had been assigned to a pair of rooms right next to each other. Snail, Eamon, and Du-Juan were in one room—Teri, Christina, and Juliana were in the other. Since they would stay together as a team underwater, being able to start each diving day side by side at the hotel was very convenient.

Although Professor Garcia was going to be leading the dive team, he was still excited for the students who were on the hiking team. They would be taking an ecological walking tour through one of the native villages this afternoon and a different one in the morning. He swept his arm across the horizon.

"There are three hundred and seventy-eight islands located north of Panama facing the Caribbean Sea and taking up only about one hundred square miles. Most of the islands have been and remain uninhabited. The natives are known as Kunas. They live on five of the major islands. They are very warm and wonderful people, who live by very strict tribal laws. For example, their laws prohibit the Kuna to marry outside of their tribe. You will notice most women wear nose rings, metal ear disks, and necklaces made of coins and beads, and they paint black lines on their noses to make them look longer. Please don't stare at the Kunas. This is considered quite rude. Just remember, this is their custom. Please respect it.

"You may take pictures of the houses and surroundings, but please do not take any pictures of the locals. If you want their picture, you must first ask permission. Their reluctance to have their pictures taken goes back many decades when someone told them if their picture was taken then their soul would also be taken, and we don't want that. So please, ask first. By the way, the villagers also have molas and other fine artifacts that may be purchased. I am sure you will enjoy your tour."

After lunch, the six diving students received their briefing on their scheduled underwater activities.

"We will leave for the marina shortly," Professor Garcia explained. "The trip to the dive site takes about thirty minutes, depending on the weather, and right now it looks great. Our boat is called the *Angel de Azul,* or Blue Angel. It is a fifty-footer and has all the comforts we need. Tanks and all the supplies are already aboard as we have used this captain in the past and he knows exactly what to do. He is very good and knows these waters well.

"We will be taking a drive along the Chagres River to catch the dive boat. If you remember your pirate history that is the same river Morgan took to Balboa as he headed toward Panama City."

The *Angel de Azul* was a clean boat but old. The captain's name was Benito, and he could have passed for a pirate. He wore a sleeveless, ripped shirt, oil-stained trousers, and dirty tennis shoes. His dark brown face was covered with a river of wrinkles from years of too much sun. His mustache looked like a long, hairy caterpillar, ungroomed and gnarly. He greeted the students with a broad smile that was welcoming, but nearly toothless. When all the divers were seated, he cranked up the engine and made his way out of the marina toward their destination. It was mid-afternoon and the weather was warm with few clouds floating by.

On the way to the dive site, Professor Garcia told them to keep an eye out for various popular marine mammals.

"In our waters we have the American manatee, whales—both blue and killer whales, and dolphins. You may see any number of these creatures as we get closer to the San Blas Islands."

The group wasn't disappointed. They were soon entertained by a huge manta ray lazily swimming near the surface. Captain Benito slowed the boat down for the students to get a better look and to take a few pictures. What they saw was amazing.

There were dozens of rays at the surface, swimming along lazily like a family out on a summer stroll.

"The giant manta ray can grow to measure over thirty feet in wingspan," Professor Garcia informed them. "By the way, the manta ray is also called the 'devil ray' here in Panama, because during mating season it has been known to come completely out of the water and land on small boats, sinking them."

"Well, none of these ones seemed to be in any sort of hurry," Eamon said. "Maybe they're just out sunbathing."

Shortly after the boat passed the rays, Benito said it was time to get ready to dive. When directed, his one crewmember dropped the anchor, waited for it to hit the bottom, and then secured it to some rocks.

"I think the water is not too cold," he said in accented English, "so no need for wet suits."

"That's cool," Snail said as he hoisted up his buoyancy compensator, commonly referred to as a BC. He checked the regulator for easy breathing, then he placed the mouthpiece in his mouth and inhaled. He received air on demand. It worked perfectly. He then helped Teri with hers.

"There are lots of sharks in the area," Garcia warned, "but then there are sharks everywhere. We will be diving on an old Spanish galleon. The wreck is about two hundred years old. It sank during a storm, and is resting in about sixty feet of water. I don't think you will find any treasure on it but the galleon is in relatively good condition for being underwater this long. Stay in your group and enjoy the dive."

"Is there anything else we need to know about sharks?"

Eamon asked.

"Yes, remember sharks are sensitive to sound. They can hear farther than they can see. What will catch their attention are low frequency sounds that are out of the ordinary. The sounds created by an animal thrashing or making struggling sounds are what draws the shark's attention. Once the shark senses this, it quickly surmises something in distress and follows the sounds."

Although nothing had seemed unusual to the students as they headed out to the dive site, there were some extra eyes watching the *Angel de Azul* pull away. Vega, Nuñez, Lorino, and de Costa were now aboard an old decrepit cabin cruiser called the *Renegade Runner*. It followed a few minutes after the *Angel de Azul* left port. The wreck they were in was a dirty beat-up mess, but it still floated and it was fast.

"Maintain a safe distance behind Benito's boat until he stops and drops anchor," Vega instructed the captain, Mr. Salazar. "The rest of you get your gear on."

They followed behind the larger boat, and eventually Vega watched the *Angel de Azul* slow down and stop.

"Slow down and pass by," he ordered Salazar.

The *Renegade Runner* traveled about another two hundred yards, then stopped and dropped anchor. Vega watched as the students entered the water, then ordered his men to dive.

The students entered individually. Just as Benito had said,

the water was warm. Each student entered the water, gave the international sign by placing one hand on their head, indicating that everything was fine, and waited for everyone to gather at the anchor line. From there they proceeded downward to the wreck.

Taking their time, they approached from the bow of the wreck and made their way around the ship looking at the vast quantity of fish that had gathered for lunch, feeding on the smaller fish and plankton. The galleon rested at an angle against an outcrop of large rocks that hid the view toward the far side of the river. A few curious hammerhead sharks were circling, apparently wanting to accompany them on the dive.

The water was still clear as they went deeper. As soon as they were near the bottom, Snail spotted a gigantic sea urchin that seemed to be rolling over to where they were located. He pointed it out to his friends, and they watched as it rolled by.

Teri took a couple of pictures of it before she focused her attention on the galleon. As a pair Snail and Teri swam up to the hull, followed it around to the other side, and then ascended to the top of the ship to view it from above. She took some great photos and even got a few of Snail. There were dozens of angelfish, along with some tropical wrasse. There were also plenty of lobsters hiding in the sea grasses and rock crevices.

As they were passing the port side of the galleon, Snail suddenly noticed a group of four men emerging from behind the large outcrop of rocks, just yards away from where Teri was snapping photos.

Professor Garcia and the others were invisible beyond the

galleon's stern. Snail and Teri were alone. The four men gestured emphatically to each other, and the nearest reached out to grab Teri from behind.

Kidnappers! Snail smacked aside the man's arm, then pressed his own hand against Teri and pushed her out of the way. He then grabbed the man's arm and aggressively spun him around. Without hesitation Snail ripped off the attacker's mask. The force of Snail's attack yanked the man's mouthpiece clear out of his mouth, taking two front teeth with it in a cloud of blood. Snail grabbed the rubber tubing and ripped it free from the regulator. The man scrambled to swim clear, desperately reaching for his backup air hose. A second attacker closed in, but Snail punched out with a four-finger jab to the throat. The man flailed backward, grabbing his throat as bubbles surged around his face.

The commotion finally caught Professor Garcia's attention. He halted the student divers and swam over to intercept one of the other two attackers. Garcia tried to grapple him but the attacker pulled a knife and swiped it across the professor's shoulder. Blood poured from the wound, and everyone knew that was like ringing the dinner bell for the sharks.

Eamon swam up behind the third man and turned off his air supply at the regulator then held on to him. With no air, the man panicked, fought off Eamon's grip, and headed toward the surface. That left only one, and he was going for Christina. Snail pumped his flippers and churned through the water. He intercepted the intruder before he was able to get his hands on her, but Snail failed to see the blade.

The man swung around and Snail caught the flash of the knife mere inches from his face. He grabbed the man by the wrist and twisted it as hard as he could. The attacker dropped his knife and began kicking out with his finned feet, trying to knock Snail away and release his wrist. Snail was far too strong and maintained his iron grip on the man's wrist. He twisted it until it came around behind the man's back. Snail held on to the man's wrist with one hand and grabbed hold of the regulator with the other.

Once Snail had the man under control he looked around and saw Teri with Juliana attending to Professor Garcia. The cloud of blood from his shoulder was growing. Snail saw the large number of sharks that had gathered, circling the students. Snail, while still maintaining control of the attacker, gathered the other divers together around the bleeding professor, got his bearings, and headed slowly toward the surface, keeping a constant lookout for any aggressive sharks.

Twice sharks swam through the huddle of students but kept going without stopping. One swam close to Du-Juan and scraped his leg with its sandpaper skin. Du-Juan started to panic, but Eamon grasped Du-Juan's shoulders and calmed him enough that they could continue their ascent.

Cautiously the group of divers arrived at the boat and pushed Professor Garcia on board. Juliana, who was an Emergency Medical Technician, went next.

As the last of the students boarded, the intruder made an unexpected and aggressive move and got free from Snail's grip. He swam away as fast as he could. Snail was not willing to go after the man, especially with the number of sharks swimming nearby. Snail was the last to board the boat. He heard engines start up, and got back on deck in time to see a second boat pull away. Eamon said he saw the dorsal fins of a couple of sharks heading toward the fleeing man, but he thought he had made it out.

They headed back to port, as Professor Garcia was growing pale and weak from his injury.

Chapter 11

Captain Salazar headed his *Renegade Runner* back to dock as quickly as he could. He wanted to drop off his passengers and get far away from the area before Benito and his group of students returned. All the way back, the other men argued over their failure to capture one single girl.

"Mr. Chang is going to be angry with you all," Salazar said.

"He can be angry all he wants," Vega said as he spat out a mouth full of blood from his missing teeth. "Chang didn't say anything about having to fight off some crazy kid."

Vega was a man who would do anything for a buck, but he was angry for not being forewarned on how Snail would react. He rubbed his face and spat out another mouthful of blood. "I will get even with that kid."

Looking around at the other men, he noticed that de Costa's

throat was bruised and his voice sounded raspy, and Nuñez was complaining that he nearly drowned from some kid turning off his air supply.

Lorino was sitting quietly was after having been nearly eaten by the sharks. "That kid nearly broke my arm, I am going to get even with him before any of you other guys do. I promise that."

"When we get back to shore," Salazar said, "you get off this boat as fast as you can. I don't want you near me or my boat again. Do you understand?"

"But Chang will find you," Vega warned. "You cannot hide from him."

"He won't find me. I am leaving Panama and going to … Never mind. That's not important. I'm leaving and he won't find me."

There was worried silence aboard the *Renegade Runner*, as she was running at top speed toward the port. As soon as the boat pulled close to the dock, Vega and his three companions tossed their equipment from the boat, then leaped off and ran to their van. The moment they were off the boat, the captain put the boat in reverse and cleared out.

The San Blas hospital that Professor Garcia visited was more like a rural clinic. It was a dirty white single-story structure with a single doctor, two nurses, and an orderly. They did have a portable x-ray machine that the doctor operated when necessary, and a small laboratory to run some tests.

The doctor, who introduced himself as Dr. Emilio de la Cruz, examined Professor Garcia's shoulder and complimented Juliana's first aid. Professor Garcia spent about an hour being examined and sewed up before he was given permission to leave.

Dr. de la Cruz escorted Professor Garcia from the emergency room, where they were met by the two police officers who had been dispatched to interview Snail and the other divers. Snail and Eamon had given the police an accurate account of what happened but were unable to provide any description of the assailants. One police officer, who spoke fairly decent English, was able to ask the important questions and understand the young mens' responses. Professor Garcia was interviewed but had nothing more to add to what the police had already been told. Before the police allowed them to leave, they went over their notes with the professor in Spanish, making sure everything was correct. Once the police left to file their report, the students returned to the hotel.

"The police in Panama are like most other law enforcement agencies worldwide—under paid, over worked, and in serious need of training. Our men and women do a good job at with what they have, but could use some additional training."

Eamon asked, "What would happen if you requested some training for them in LA? Think that would work?"

"I'm not sure if it would help or not. That type of request needs to come from the police commissioner in Panama to the commissioner in Los Angeles. I could recommend it, but who knows if it would help."

Later that evening with his arm now in a sling, Professor

Garcia came into the hotel lobby and announced that they would be leaving early the next morning.

"Because of the incident today, we're going to curtail our activities here and move to the Pacific side of the country. We don't know who those men are and it would be wise to put as much distance between us and them as we can."

Snail spoke up. "Professor, that was actually the second attempt on us. The other day, when we had gone into town to pick up water, we were threatened by three men, but we stopped them in what ever it was they were trying to do. I initially thought it was a simple robbery, a couple of guys going after some tourists, but now, I'm not so sure."

"This is worrying." Professor Garcia addressed the entire group. "From now on whenever you go into town or leave the university grounds please travel in pairs, let someone know where you are going, and be careful. If you have to run for your lives, then do it. No one is going to blame you for running away from a crime. I do not want anyone here harmed in any way. Is that perfectly clear?"

All the students agreed.

Du-Juan said that he was thankful Snail was able to take care of the men. "I was really scared," he admitted. "I didn't know what was happening down there. It all happened so fast. Thanks, Snail."

"Yeah, no problem Du-Juan." Snail's tone, although he didn't mean to be, was not pleasant. He sat down next to Teri.

"Something about that guy Du-Juan drives me nuts. He knows something. I just don't know what."

Chapter 12

By mid-afternoon, after driving like maniacs through the jungle, Vega and his men finally arrived in Panama City. They were dreading their meeting with Chang.

They feared Chang would be furious when he discovered that the kids got away. But he was remarkably calm, considering what had happened. He glared at them each in turn.

"Explain how they were able to escape, and were able to do this," he gestured to de Costa's bruises and Vega's missing teeth, "to you when there were four of you."

"I think it was the kid you wanted us to stop," Vega replied. "You never said how strong or fast he was. He attacked me when I was going for the girl."

"That boy is smart, and strong. And based on your efforts it appears that kidnapping the girl cleanly is too difficult a task.

At least you've scared them—even causing them that small bit of suffering makes your failure acceptable."

Vega glanced at the others. Chang's cruel attitude was enough to chill the blood.

"Let me tell you what I have just found out," Chang continued.

The four men took seats and waited for Chang to continue.

"One of my informants told me that the students will be making another dive later this week off Balboa. You will be there and this time you will succeed." Chang gave them the information that had been provided by Du-Juan.

"Tomorrow evening, Vega and I are going to the dine at the Ego y Narcisco restaurant. That is the same restaurant where the students will be dining. My contact will meet me there, and I will give him directions on how to get to this building. Vega, at dinner you will learn exactly what your two targets look like. You are responsible for making sure that, on the next dive, neither of them comes out of the water alive." Chang smiled fiendishly at Vega. "Now, get yourself to the dentist and see if he can do something about those missing teeth. Make sure you are back here by six tomorrow evening, clean and ready to go to dinner."

"Yes, Mr. Chang."

"You two," Chang pointed at de Costa and Lorino, "get yourselves ready to go to Balboa and remain near your phone in case I need to get in touch with you."

Chang took a deep breath before he continued.

"You will succeed this time, or you won't be coming back.

Now get out of here."

The mood on the bus was tense, as some students discussed the sudden and mysterious attack, while others tried to forget about it. Du-Juan remained silent as the students discussed the attack in whispered tones. When asked about it, Du-Juan just shrugged his shoulders and remained as silent as a church mouse.

Snail watched Du-Juan's withdrawn behavior and knew that something was definitely wrong.

"When we return to the dorm," he whispered to Teri, "I'm going to get Du-Juan off by himself and have a little heart-to-heart chat with him. He knows something and I need to know what."

Back at the university dormitory, Du-Juan made it a point to stay clear of Snail and his friends. Peeking out of his door, Du-Juan saw that the coast was clear, with no students milling around. Not wanting to be overheard by anyone, he stepped silently out the door, fled the dorm, and found an empty office to use his cell phone and call Chang. He had more details about the upcoming dive, but he felt he needed to know more about what Chang's plans were. He couldn't shake the feeling that the attack yesterday hadn't been as random as the other students thought.

"No, I understand," Chang said on the line, "don't worry. I will be at the restaurant tonight, but Du-Juan, you must remain silent when you see me. I don't want them realizing that we know each other. It would spoil my … publication plans."

Despite the reassuring words, Chang's tone was brash and unpleasant. Du-Juan didn't know if it was because of the current situation or if that was just Chang's normal tone. Either way, it bothered him. But he pressed on.

"There is something else you need to know," he said.

"And what is that?"

"Professor Garcia mentioned the other day there was, in addition to the golden altar, a treasure that had been hidden from the invading pirates somewhere on Cathedral Tower grounds. Morgan and his men didn't find this treasure. I'm not sure if it's still there or not. Garcia didn't know for sure."

"Good, keep me informed on this, Du-Juan. If there is a treasure hidden in the cathedral …" Chang trailed off, a hungry tone to his voice.

"It would make a good story," Du-Juan offered.

"… Yes." Without another word, the line went dead.

Du-Juan didn't know what to think. He was worried Chang might have had something to do with putting his life in danger earlier.

When Du-Juan was returning to his dorm room, he spotted Snail coming back from the kitchen area. Du-Juan stopped when he saw Snail approaching.

"Hey, Du-Juan, where ya been?" Snail asked.

"Just out taking a stroll. I felt like I needed some fresh air.

What's up?"

"Actually, I wanted to speak with you about the attack yesterday. I could tell by your comment that you were scared. Heck, we were all scared, and there's nothing to be ashamed about. We, Teri, me, and Christina are really concerned about you."

"I was afraid I might get hurt."

"I understand no one wants to get hurt. But what about the other students, the girls who were being attacked, and Professor Garcia? Didn't you think about them?"

"I don't think they like me. I can tell when I come into a room everyone stops talking."

Snail didn't know what to say at that moment. He was stunned by Du-Juan's comment.

"Look, Du-Juan, maybe it's not them liking you as much as it is the way you're acting."

"What do you mean?"

"It's almost as if you don't want people to talk to you. You are very quiet, almost standoffish. Look, I heard Juliana tell Teri that she thinks you're good looking. I think she likes you but you have to be a bit more friendly and available to her and the other students."

Du-Juan didn't respond, but Snail could tell something else was bothering him.

"Du-Juan, tell me what it is and maybe I can help out. I'm not going to beg you to spill your guts to me; I just want to know if there is anything I can do, that's all."

Again Du-Juan remained silent for a few moments. He

looked at Snail, wondering what was really going on in his mind. Did he really want to help or was he just being nosey? Du-Juan took a deep breath.

"Look, Snail, I believe you, and I do have some issues that I'm trying to get squared away. I don't really think you can do anything about it, but I appreciate your asking."

"Okay, if that's what you want. Look, Teri, Eamon, Christina, and Juliana are also worried about you. That's all. We're not the enemy here, we're trying to be your friend if you allow us to be." Snail put his hands on Du-Juan's shoulders.

"Thanks." He tried to keep himself from trembling.

"Okay, see you at dinner later?"

"Fine, see you there." Du-Juan stepped away and returned to his room, leaving Snail in the hallway.

Watching Du-Juan leave, Snail was more convinced than ever that he was hiding something. But he let it go for now and returned to his room, where Eamon was sitting with Teri and Christina. He told them about his chat with Du-Juan.

"He's certainly afraid of something. He was shaking like a leaf when I put my hands on his shoulders. It was definitely fear. Something or someone has threatened Du-Juan. Keep an eye on him this evening at dinner. He's bound to let some nugget of truth slip out. I know he will."

The aromas of the Ego y Narcisco restaurant filled the air. They were mouth-watering, and the students hadn't even ordered yet.

"Wow, something smells wonderful." Eamon said. "Nothing smells like that in Ireland, that's for sure."

"We ate here a couple of days ago, and the food was fabulous," Christina said as she rubbed her empty tummy. "I can't wait to try some shrimp and pineapple tapas."

One long table had been set up for the students and Professor Garcia, who was accompanied by his wife Gabriella.

Gabriella wanted to know more about the attack on the wreck and how her husband was injured. Professor Garcia downplayed the event and suggested the attackers were probably some punk kids who thought they could do something dangerous and get away with it.

"Well, they did get away, but they succeeded in doing nothing except cutting me. Our expert EMT Juliana fixed me up, and all is well. The incident is behind us, so let's enjoy our tapas and the evening."

The entertainment for the evening was two flamenco dancers with long flowing red and black dresses, black scarves, and high heels. Accompanying the dancers were two guitarists and one male singer.

Everyone engaged in friendly chatter as they appreciated the delightful taste of tapas with shrimp, eggplant, mango, pork, fish, and coconut. The portions were small but the flavor was incredible. On one occasion, Snail glanced over at Du-Juan to see if he was enjoying himself. He wasn't. Juliana had seated herself next to him so she could talk to him and help him relax, but it didn't seem to be doing much good.

Fifteen minutes after the tapas were served, two men entered the restaurant and took a table not too far from the students. When Du-Juan saw them he stiffened, and his eyes followed them to their seats. Snail saw this.

The shorter of the two men sported long hair, a long mustache and wore sunglasses. The second walked with a confident swagger, but his face and lips were a bit swollen. Snail had seen enough football players get hit in the face to recognize an injury, probably to his mouth.

Snail watched Du-Juan for some time as his eyes never left the two men who had just entered. Snail felt in his gut that these two men had something to do with the way Du-Juan was acting. Pretending to stretch his back, Snail twisted in his chair first in one direction then the other wanting to get a better look at the men. He didn't recognize them, but one did look strangely familiar.

Suddenly, the smaller of the two men stood up and left the table, heading toward the men's room. Du-Juan hesitated for a few seconds, then politely excused himself and stepped away. Snail watched Du-Juan leave, then looked at Eamon and nodded. Eamon stood and strolled behind Du-Juan and followed him into the men's room.

When he emerged a few minutes later, he whispered to Snail, telling him what he saw.

"When I entered the men's room after Du-Juan, I noticed the long-haired man attempting to give something to Du-Juan, who quickly withdrew his hand. Du-Juan then said, 'Sorry mister, but I can't help you.' The long-haired man then left."

"I think we need to have another chat with Du-Juan," Snail said.

Eamon nodded, his gaze lifting quickly to look at the table where the long-haired man had retaken his seat.

"And you know what else?" he said. "That other man, he looks familiar, Snail, but from where I have no idea."

"I think the man with long hair looks familiar," Teri said, leaning in to join the whispered conversation. "There's something about him."

Snail looked at the two men.

"The smaller one kind of resembles Chang in size and walk. Chang had short hair, no mustache, and doesn't wear glasses, but this man does look Chinese."

"You two have mentioned this man Chang before," Christina said. "If I may ask, who is he?"

"Chang is a ruthless, murdering dirt bag," Teri blurted, then stopped.

Snail finished what she had started, telling their friends briefly about the murder of Teri's parents, his involvement on Ocracoke Island with a Blackbeard impersonator, and on the bayou of Louisiana. When he had finished, they had a very good idea of just how bad Chang really was.

They heard laughter and turned to see the man with long hair fling his head back at something funny. That is when his hair uncovered his ear. The top part was gone.

"That's not Chang," Teri said. "He has both of his ears."

Just then, Du-Juan walked past their table and the Chinese man very quickly placed something in Du-Juan's hand. Du-Juan immediately placed the item in his pocket before re-taking his seat at the student table.

"That man handed something to Du-Juan," Eamon whispered. "A few minutes ago they were strangers, and now they're friends? Something isn't cool with this."

"I wonder if Du-Juan is in trouble?" Snail mused.

When the dinner was finally over, Du-Juan left the group and caught a taxi to the address Chang had just provided him. He knew the restaurant was located near the Plaza Bolivar and he needed to get to Plaza Herrera. His note directed him to go to the Plaza Herrera and look for the statue of General Tomás de Herrera. Next to the statue was an old building with a large porch and palm trees in the front. *Wait at the front steps for someone to collect you.* He followed the directions to the letter.

He waited a good half an hour before a middle-aged man, someone he did not recognize, came out and addressed him by name. Du-Juan, afraid like never before, was escorted up to the third floor. The man opened the door and Du-Juan was told to go inside. Nervously he entered the room and found Chang sitting there with six very unpleasant looking men. He thought he recognized three from the San Blas dive, including Vega.

"Sit down Du-Juan."

He sat without saying a word. He listened to Chang describe what he wanted done to Teri and Snail and that bothered him. When Chang finished giving directions to his men, he turned to Du-Juan.

"What information do you have for us?"

Du-Juan, too frightened to resist, gave the information he had about the upcoming dive trip to Balboa and where the students would be staying.

Chang seemed pleased with what he heard. He dismissed Du-Juan and told him to return to the dorm. "Don't speak with anyone, do you understand?"

Through trembling lips he said, "I don't think I can go through with this, Mr. Chang."

Chang was surprised to hear this. He glared at Du-Juan then said, "What are you saying, Du-Juan? You agreed to do what I needed you to do. Now you are saying you don't think you are able to do it?"

For the first time in his life Du-Juan was really scared. Listening to the way Chang spoke frightened him. He didn't understand Chang's feelings toward Teri and Snail, but they appeared deep-rooted. Du-Juan didn't want any part of any foul play, especially murder. Chang had never specifically mentioned anything about killing, but now his classmates had been officially targeted. And yet, he couldn't financially afford to disobey Chang. Not to mention what the cruel man would do to him if he found out. What was he supposed to do?

Chapter 14

The rain had not let up and many of the roads leading to the west coast from Panama City were flooded. This delay didn't dampen the spirits of the students.

Professor Garcia had directed the students to stand by in the dormitory lounge and keep their bags close by.

"The bus driver has gone to the police station to see what roads are passable and which ones are not. Once he figures out a suitable route, we are out of here. Stay close; we may have a very short window of opportunity to move."

Like most kids who have to wait, they slept. Some of the boys used their backpacks as pillows and slept on the floor. Some of the girls slept on the couches or chairs. Everyone seemed relaxed, even Du-Juan, who had been speaking more frequently and friendlier with Juliana, which was a big change. Snail saw this as a good sign. But it bothered him at the same time. He watched Du-Juan acting differently than the day before.

Sitting next to Teri, Snail asked, "Have you noticed a difference in Du-Juan's behavior?"

"Yes, I have. He seems to be a different person today. What did you say to him?"

"I just said we were worried about him. I wonder if the talk sunk in and he's now going to be friendlier."

"Well, I hope so."

"But I question if something happened last night when he darted from the restaurant and disappeared for a couple of hours."

While they were waiting, Professor Garcia let them know a little bit about what to expect in their coming trip to the Darién region.

"I am from the Guna tribe, one of the many tribes that reside in the Darién region of Panama. The Guna were known for helping British and French pirates by providing them with safe harbor and shelter from the Spanish." Pausing for a moment, he then said, "The Guna people were also known as headhunters.

"My father was responsible for relocating me to Panama City as a young child so I could be properly educated. I lived with my aunt and her family in the Canal Zone and went to an international school there. That is where I learned English. At the international school I learned about the many cultures of the world. Most of the students were children of diplomats that were serving in Panama or their parents worked for one of many international businesses located throughout the city.

"I still maintain contact with my family and other members of my tribe and correspond with them on a regular basis. My visits with them are as frequent as I can make them."

The bus driver soon returned, reporting that the main road to Balboa was open and that they should leave immediately. Professor Garcia called out and the students headed to the bus, blurry eyed but ready for the trip. Through a constant drizzle the students jogged out to the bus and loaded up. The driver set out for Balboa.

The drive usually took an hour or two, but with the high water the driver had to maneuver carefully over the muddy roads. He drove slowly and cautiously, and the drive took over three hours. Occasionally children could be seen playing in the rain; some were even showering. The countryside looked clean and inviting. The temperature was comfortable right now, but when the rain stopped the humidity would take off and everyone would be sticky and hot.

The hotel in Balboa was small but comfortable. At dinner that night, Professor Garcia was met by some of his family members and their friends. He introduced them to the students but said that their dialect was not a common one; so speaking with them would be difficult.

"Just smile and say 'hi'. They all understand that."

The Guna were all very friendly. They were small in stature.

None was over five and a half feet tall, and no one weighed much more than maybe 130 pounds.

"The women are very attractive," Christina said. "They have very fine facial features." She stopped talking as she took in their beauty. "They are all so tanned, they look more like porcelain dolls, very delicate."

Each woman wore attractive ear ornaments and sported nose rings. The men were muscular and had tattoos covering their arms, chests, and backs.

Snail said, "The tattoos look good on them, but I don't personally care for tattoos. You know, in Hawaii the local men have tattoos. But I don't know; it just ain't my thing."

Chapter 15

The bus arrived at the port of Balboa by noon and the six student divers were introduced to the captain, Alonzo Delgado, a short, stocky muscular man with tattoos running up and down both arms, a bandito mustache, and a pleasant smile. When he saw Professor Garcia the smile grew even larger.

"*Buenas tardes. Bienvenido a Balboa y mi barco* La Paloma Blanca." In very broken English he said, "Welcome to Balboa and my boat *The White Dove.*"

He then said something to Garcia, who smiled and beckoned the students to board. *The White Dove* was a clean forty-footer with a small galley and a smaller bathroom. There were a few well-used deck chairs, which the students quickly occupied.

Once the equipment, suitcases, and students were loaded on board, Alonzo started up the engines, and his crewman untied the bowline. Alonzo expertly guided the boat away from the dock and out to sea. The coastal water was light blue and incredibly calm. The clouds were white and fluffy with no sight of rain on the horizon. It was a beautiful day for a boat ride and dive.

The other students who did not dive took a second boat that followed Captain Alonzo. They were going to the ranger station to embark on an ecological walking tour that would last two days. They were excited knowing that they were going to see some exotic animals and birds.

"Captain Alonzo speaks almost no English," explained Professor Garcia, "but he is a first-class dive master. When underwater he will use hand and arm signals."

Alonzo spoke to Garcia for a minute, pointing at the chart.

"The captain says we will be traveling past Taboga and Sobata Islands," Garcia translated, "and spending the night in the Coiba National Park. You will find it a beautiful location with lots to see. But there are some things you need to know first."

Du-Juan asked, "What do you mean 'know first'? Is it dangerous?"

"No, not today, but it was at one time. The island was originally a penal colony. Really bad people were sent there. The area is considered a restricted area; firstly is because the island was a penal colony; secondly is because there are rumors that the famed ship, *La Santissima Trinidata,* rests off one of the island. It has never been found so it is just a rumor. And thirdly, there has been an increase in illegal drugs entering Panama from

South America. This is a big no-no in Panama as drugs are not allowed. Therefore, we need a pass to enter the area, and that is why I have Captain Alonzo as our guide. He travels here often and knows his way around. Since we are an educational group, we will be allowed to dive in otherwise restricted areas. We will be staying the night at the ANAM—the National Authority for the Environment ranger station. They have a few modest two-room cabins that have been reserved for us."

Alonzo said something, and he and the professor had an exchange that lasted for a couple of minutes. Finally, Garcia translated.

"Captain Alonzo says that when we dive, don't be surprised to see a whale shark or two. They frequent these waters. Also, be cautious of other sharks and predators."

Alonzo guided the boat out of the Bay of Panama toward the Gulf of Panama that connected with the Pacific Ocean. The water was calm, the sun was high in the sky, and the warmth of the air was pleasant. The kids all settled down and watched as the city of Balboa disappeared, and the various islands on the western horizon came into view. They knew this was going to be a great diving adventure.

Snail and Teri were holding hands and talking about the upcoming dive when Eamon came over with Christina and sat down next to them.

"Snail, I've had my eye on Du-Juan since we left the city," Eamon said, "and I'm not sure what's going on with him. He has been overly quiet and deliberately avoiding everyone. On the bus he and Juliana were talking, and he seemed happy, but now he won't speak with her. She's the most social one in the group, and now he even avoids her. Something ain't right."

The four of them looked over to where Du-Juan was sitting, alone and away from everyone.

Snail went up to Du-Juan.

"Hey, Du-Juan," he said in as friendly a tone as he could manage, "can I sit down with you?"

"Why?" Du-Juan's posture and expression suggested that something was seriously wrong.

"We're all worried about you. Is there anything I can do to help?"

"No, there is nothing you can do, Snail. You shouldn't be concerned with me. I'm all right. I just prefer to be alone. I like my solitude."

"That's not it. There's something else going on. Everyone can see that there's something bothering you. If it's school, there are people who can help."

"And if it's not school, are there still people to help?" Du-Juan asked.

"That depends on what that something is, I guess."

Du-Juan looked like he wanted to say more, but he seemed afraid. Snail tried another tactic.

"Why don't you hang out with Juliana? She kind of likes you, I think."

Du-Juan's body remained as stiff as ever, but he took a deep breath. "Yeah, I think you're probably right, Snail. I have been distracted lately and need to be part of the class. Juliana's really nice—I'll talk to her."

"I think that's a great idea." Snail tapped Du-Juan on the shoulder and could feel the shakiness and tenseness when he did.

The boat trip to Coiba National Park took a couple of hours. They were met at the dock by a young ranger working with the National Authority for the Environment. His short-sleeved khaki uniform was neatly pressed and ironed. He escorted the class from the dock to their assigned rooms.

In less than an hour, Captain Alonzo had *The White Dove* heading out toward San Jose Island for their latest wreck dive. While Professor Garcia could not dive due to his injuries, he noted that the captain and his crewman were both excellent divers.

"Captain Alonzo will lead the dive this afternoon, and his crewman Hector will also dive as a safety precaution. I have known them for years, and they are both very good divers and quite knowledgeable of the area. We will be at the site in about thirty minutes, so start getting your equipment together. Let's be ready when the anchor goes down."

"What ship are we going to dive on, Professor?" asked Teri.

"The wreck we are diving on this afternoon is another Spanish galleon. We are not one-hundred percent sure of its name since it went down over three hundred years ago, but most of the hull and deck are still intact. From what the captain tells me, this may have been one of the galleons that was used to transport conquistadores north into Mexico. It supposedly sank, like so many other ships on the Pacific side, as a result of a storm. No one really knows for sure. I dove on it once and was impressed by its size. We are only guessing now but there may be doubloons, Spanish gold coins, on the ship."

"I see a fin following our boat," Snail said. "Does that mean there are lots of sharks down there, or is this one looking for a handout?"

"Yes, there are a number of sharks down there, including Mako, hammerheads, white and black tip sharks, just to name a few. Hector will have a spear gun with him just in case one gets a little too aggressive."

Snail looked at Du-Juan and immediately picked up on his nervousness.

"I bet he doesn't stay down that long once he sees how many sharks are present in these waters," he whispered to Teri. "We need him to stay with Juliana. We need to place ourselves so close to him that every time he moves, we're there. Just in case he decides to bolt."

With Professor Garcia translating, Captain Alonzo gave a very thorough briefing about the wreck. Everyone was excited and prepared to enter. What excited the class again was the comment Alonzo made about this ship possibly being the *La Santissima Trinidata*, the same ship the Religious claimed to have used to hide the golden alter. It supposedly sank in this area. Everyone was glad to be diving—everyone with the exception of Du-Juan. He was once again showing reluctance in diving.

The Pacific side of the Panamanian coast was far different

from the Atlantic side, with more coral, clearer waters, and lots of predators. One by one the students entered the water, gave the 'okay' signal, and proceeded to the anchor line.

Snail kept a close eye on Du-Juan. Something in his gut told him that Du-Juan was up to something. When everyone was underwater and ready, Alonzo led off and Hector followed in the rear with his spear gun—just in case.

The water was pleasant and the visibility was incredible. At ten feet below the surface, Alonzo gathered the divers and pointed out the sharks in the area. There were numerous sharks, but fortunately they kept their distance. The group continued to descend to nearly fifty feet and was just off the bottom, swimming lazily along toward the wreck. They encountered dozens of fish swimming in and out of those coral reefs.

Within ten minutes they came over a small rise and got their first view of the sunken ship. Alonzo indicated that they were going to first swim around the wreck and get a feel for the environment. If he felt it was safe enough he would then direct the students to go up to the deck and have a look around.

The wreck seemed to be in fairly good condition considering it had been underwater for nearly three centuries. Even so, the masts had long ago fallen off and the sides looked rotten and eaten away. Snail didn't think that it was a good idea to try to enter the ship; he was unsure of the integrity of the wooden sides or even the deck.

Snail made sure Du-Juan was acting in accordance with diving protocols, that he wasn't doing something stupid which would put himself or the other divers in any danger. He seemed to be okay, but as they approached the wreck, he kept looking around. This suspicious action bothered Snail. He continued to watch him and his partner Juliana, making sure she was safe.

The divers approached the boat with caution as sharks and moray eels were known to hide inside of wrecks. Alonzo led the group up to the port side and examined it, then motioned for the divers to follow him. They swam around the stern of the ship, looking to see if the name was still present, but unfortunately it had long disappeared. Once they had gone around the ship, Alonzo motioned for the divers to look for any artifacts that might be hiding in the sandy bottom. He did this by running his fingers through the sand and letting it sift through his fingers.

His directions were easy to follow and all the divers started doing the same thing. Usually on an old wreck that had been dove on many times, there would be nothing to find as other divers would have already searched the area and taken what they could. But good fortune was on their side. This had been a restricted dive spot so it was less explored. Juliana ran her fingers through the sandy bottom and, to Snail's surprise, she pulled out a small handful of pieces of eight that had become stuck together with sea life after many years underwater. She picked up the bundle of coins and examined them carefully. She pointed excitedly to the surface of the coins. Snail recognized the Spanish writing, and knew she had found something really cool. She tugged on Du-Juan's fin to get his attention and show him what she found. He seemed to be genuinely delighted and gave her a fist-bump.

There was an abundance of sea creatures near the wreck. The surrounding area had sea urchins galore, moray eels with their heads peeking out of their sandy homes. No one else found anything of interest until Eamon and Christina drifted a short distance away from the group and began searching the surrounding area. As they were about to return to the group, Eamon pointed to an object in the distance, and he and Christina swam over to it. Snail couldn't see what it was, but after a moment Eamon swam back over and got Snail and Teri to follow him back. He pointed at the find, which Christina was still floating beside, and motioned for them to help him. Carefully they all examined it. Snail noted that it was at least six feet long and resting in an awkward position. The smaller end was facing toward the surface and the larger end was stuck in a rocky crevice. It looked like a cannon. Eamon took hold to see if he could wiggle it loose. It was definitely stuck fast. All four struggled to move it, but the cannon wasn't moving.

Clearly disappointed, Eamon shrugged his shoulders. Snail, though, had seen something similar when they found Thomas Doughty's dinghy. That time they had had to use a hammer to break the debris free from the rocks, and then employed a net and pulley to bring it up. Snail gave the 'okay' signal to Eamon indicating that he knew how to recover the cannon. They got their bearings from the wreck to make it easier to find on the next dive.

The four divers returned to the wreck and noticed that Du-Juan and Juliana had gathered close around Hector. He was sitting on the sandy bottom cradling something in his lap.

Upon closer examination, it looked like a ship's bell. Ship's bells were priceless, as the name of the vessel would be inscribed on it. Some even had the date the ship was christened. It was pretty corroded, but it was an amazing find.

Alonzo pointed to his watch and indicated it was time to ascend to the surface. Snail tugged on Eamon's arm and pointed in the direction of the cannon to suggest that he tell the captain what he and Christina found. Eamon acknowledged and swam over to Alonzo pointing in the direction from which they had just come. The captain nodded his head, and the entire group followed Eamon.

Eamon led the group and stopped beside his find. Alonzo and Hector both surveyed the object, before giving the 'okay' signal. He patted Eamon on the shoulder then directed everyone to head back to *The White Dove*.

With the cautionary stop of three minutes at fifteen feet, the divers were all back aboard *The White Dove* in ten minutes. Excitement was on everyone's face. Professor Garcia was happy when he saw the pieces of eight and the ship's bell. He was even more excited when he learned of the cannon. But Captain Alonzo dashed all the happiness when he announced that all finds underwater in the bay were the property of the National Authority for the Environment.

"I am sorry," Professor Garcia translated, "but it is the law."

He also said that he would speak with the rangers and ask special permission for Juliana to be allowed to keep a few of the pieces of eight she found. Alonzo said that the cannon would have to be left in place, but the bell would be cleaned up and placed on display.

Alonzo directed Hector to pull up the anchor before he started up the engines. The kids had all taken seats and were unwinding from the dive.

Chapter 16

The second day of diving began with an early wake-up call followed by scrambled eggs, toast, and potatoes with fresh bananas. No acidic foods such as pineapples and mangoes were offered before the dive, as Captain Alonzo didn't want any sick divers. He had announced the day before that he wanted everyone on the boat by 8:00 a.m. so he could pull out at high tide and head for a second wreck. This one he promised was even grander than the one they had been on the day before. Again using Professor Garcia as his interpreter, Alonzo said that the last time he dove on this wreck he saw a few sights that took his breath away. His enthusiasm had the divers all excited.

When they arrived at the boat, they were informed that Hector would not be diving today; he had become sick sometime during the night. Alonzo explained to the students that the new crewman was named Manuel de Costa. "He is new to me, but is recommended by the local divers as very reliable." Professor Garcia translated as the captain spoke.

Snail eyeballed the new crewman with a degree of skepticism. He was a good-sized man, with long black curly hair and large tattoos on his forearms, one of an attacking shark and the other of pirate skull and crossbones. He also displayed tattoos on his chest, neck, and back. Snail thought they were over the top and not very well done.

When Snail shook his hand and got a good look at the man's face. He didn't like what he saw. It was Manuel's smile; there was something about it that set off an internal alarm inside the young man's brain. It looked artificial. Manuel looked familiar, but Snail couldn't remember where or if he had seen him before. Examining the face in more detail, Snail saw that he had scratch marks and bruises on his face and neck as if he had been in some sort of recent physical struggle.

As promised, by eight that morning Captain Alonzo had *The White Dove* cranked up and heading out to sea. Professor Garcia said the ride this morning was going to take ninety minutes to two hours depending on the currents.

"The wreck," he said, "rests between the Pearl Islands and Isla del Rey. There are lots of surging currents down there, and the rocks and coral reef in this area are sharp, so make sure you have your gloves on. I don't want anyone unnecessarily cut up."

The ocean heading toward the islands was rougher than the day before, and there were very few visual signs of sharks and rays in the area. Snail moved about the boat, talking cheerfully with the other divers, asking them how they felt and if they were ready to explore the new wreck. Making his way forward he stood next to Du-Juan and could sense something was amiss.

"Du-Juan, are you okay this morning? You look a bit out of sorts."

"Hey, Snail. I'm all right," he said with a weak smile. "I just didn't sleep well last night. I'm not sure why. Maybe it was the bed. It was sort of lumpy and uncomfortable. Once we get in the water and on that old wreck, I'll be just fine. But thanks for asking." Du-Juan turned and walked away before Snail could say another word.

When Snail turned around to return to Teri, he spotted Manuel talking to her. It was obvious that she was uncomfortable as she kept moving away as he kept moving closer to her. Another alarm went off in Snail's brain. He returned to Teri's side and wedged himself between her and Manuel. That was enough of a suggestion for Manuel to leave, and he did, but only after giving Snail a close once-over.

As Captain Alonzo guided *The White Dove* around Pearl Island he pointed out more manta rays on the surface. He slowed the *Dove* down so the students could get a closer look. Teri was already taking photos and got a good one of a ray leaping far out of the water and then splashing down, causing a huge ripple effect on the surface.

"Wow, that was magnificent. Snail, did you see that?"

"Yes, I did."

"The manta rays are leaping out of the water performing their mating ritual," Professor Garcia explained. "This is the season when the male finds the female, and they mate. They will have a baby and then will stay together as a family for as long as possible." There were now a number of rays leaping high into the air and doing swan dives back into the ocean.

The water between Pearl Island and Isla del Rey was much calmer than the bay, making everyone happy. Captain Alonzo was studying the landmarks on his fish finder and depth gauge when, all of a sudden, he throttled down the engines and directed Manual to get ready to drop anchor. When he found what he was looking for, he called out to Manuel to release the anchor. Once secured, Alonzo turned off the engines and had the divers gather at the stern of the boat where he gave his pre-dive instructions.

Professor Garcia interpreted Captain Alonzo's briefing.

"The wreck we are diving on this morning has been in the water for about one hundred fifty years and is still in nice shape." He displayed a diagram of the ship and showed them exactly how they would approach it. "The currents are strong here so we will approach from the stern, swimming up the starboard side and then down the port side. Once we have gone around the ship we will ascend to the deck and pass over it. On this morning's dive we will not enter the boat, but we will get a good impression of her layout, and I will show you where we will enter when we make our second dive this afternoon. Again, I must caution you about sharks and eels. Many have taken up residence inside these old wrecks, so we must be careful not to disturb them. So let's get ready. I would like to be in the water in fifteen minutes. Stay with the group just like yesterday. The only change is with Manuel; he will be following with his spear gun, keeping a close eye on the sharks to make sure they stay away from us in case one decides to get too nosey."

On the dive, Manuel tried repeatedly to get Teri away from Snail and to come to the back with him. She refused and waved her finger at him, indicating she wanted to remain with Snail. She even pointed at her ring finger and held Snail's hand. Manuel shrugged as if it were nothing and slowly drifted back to the end of the divers. But it was obvious he was more interested in Teri than the sharks.

Captain Alonzo was right; the currents were strong this morning as he carefully guided the divers around the ship. At one point Alonzo stopped and pointed at a strange creature partially covered in sand. It was an angel shark—in scientific terms it was called a *squatiniformes*. Upon closer examination the young divers could see that this shark was slightly buried on the bottom using the sand as camouflage. Only its eyes and part of the top of its body were exposed. From what they could make out, it had a flat body and a blunt nose. It lay perfectly still.

Teri took her camera, swam above the angel shark and snapped a few photos. It was nearly perfectly camouflaged. Its wide fins resembled wings; Snail figured that was how it got its name.

Alonzo swam up behind the shark and nudged it with his fin. The angel shark reacted immediately and sped off leaving a trail of sand floating in its track. As the shark swam away, the divers could see that it was about three feet long and had a large mouth similar to that of a stingray. It also sported large flat pectoral fins that extended over the gills. Its dorsal fins actually began at the base of the body where the tail begins, not in the middle of the back like most other sharks.

Also hiding in the sandy bottom were smaller stingrays and a goblin shark, often described as one of the ugliest and most bizarre looking of all living sharks. Alonzo pointed it out as soon as he spotted it. The goblin shark had a long dagger-like snout, flattened in the shape of a paddle, which extended far out in front of its mouth. Its jaws protruded prominently and when extended displayed large, slender needle-sharp teeth at the front, ideal for grasping small fish. The smaller teeth at the back formed a crushing plate for processing its captured prey. This shark had a flabby pinkish gray body which gradually grew darker as it neared the gills and on the fins. Its eyes were tiny and barely visible. Goblin sharks, while hideous to look at, were not dangerous to divers, as their main diet consisted of small fish and plankton. Teri was able to get a couple of good photos of this critter as it swam away.

The divers were amazed by these sights within the first fifteen minutes of the dive. Snail forgot about Du-Juan and concentrated on the dive.

Alonzo next led the divers toward the wreck and slowly swam around it. Snail looked at the magnificent ship as it was now and imagined how it must have been when on the surface. Once they did the circuit around the ship, Alonzo led them across the bow and deck. He was taking his time as he wanted them to see just how special this relic was. While they swam over the deck, the sudden appearance of an eel caught their attention. It was unusual for an eel to come out of its hiding place during the day, as they were nocturnal creatures, so something must have startled it. Alonzo pulled up and halted the others, waiting to see what disturbed the eel.

A few seconds later, a crocodile shark shot out of an opening. It was small, no more than two feet, and very fast. This shark, like the eel, was a night predator, so it was unusual to see one during the day. It was also unusual to see one so close to shore as it usually preferred much deeper waters. What caught everyone's attention was the shark's large eyes. They were nearly as large as its head. The crocodile shark swam up to the divers then abruptly made a turn away from them. In the shadows created by the superstructure of the wreck, the crocodile shark looked to be dark brown on top and a lighter shade of brown on the belly.

So far, this dive had everything! They had seen unusual sightings of ugly sharks, nocturnal animals venturing out during the day, and a pretty fabulous old wreck that was urging them to come inside.

Alonzo checked his watch and pointed toward the surface, indicating that it was time to head back to *The White Dove* to decompress, rest, eat, and prepare for the next dive. While heading away from the wreck, Alonzo unexpectedly stopped the group for a moment and pointed out a strange-looking creature moving along the sandy bottom heading toward the coral reef. It appeared to be a red colored starfish with not five arms but more than twenty. Upon closer examination the students noticed that the arms were multicolored with yellow, green and orange spines, the spines looked to be about two to three inches long and very sharp. And it was huge, measuring almost two feet across. Everyone watched as it made its way slowly across the sandy bottom using its many arms to propel itself.

Alonzo stopped the divers and, holding up his index finger, waved it back and forth, indicating not to touch this creature. Alonzo quickly pulled out his underwater writing pad and scribbled "peligro". Being from Southern California where the Spanish speaking population is quite large, the divers understood the meaning of "peligro"—danger.

Back on the boat, Alonzo immediately called Professor Garcia over and they had a brief chat. Then Professor Garcia summoned all the divers together, and he explained what they had just seen.

"Captain Alonzo tells me what you saw on your way back. It is called the Crown of Thorns Starfish. Its name is biblical, coming from its resemblance of the crown of thorns that were placed on Jesus' head when he was crucified. It is highly toxic and its meat is poisonous. If you touch it, that part of your body will swell up really fast, and the pain you will experience is beyond comprehension. It is extremely painful. Just like the parrotfish, they are an enormous threat to the reefs, which they eat. In fact, in Australia today the Great Barrier Reef is being destroyed by the Crown of Thorns. If you see one, even if is dead on the beach, stay clear."

Eamon asked, "Does it have any enemies?"

"The only enemy it has that I am aware of is the trumpet trident, a shellfish that is immune to its venom. Now, did you see any parrotfish?"

No one spoke up except Manuel, who said they hadn't seen any.

"The parrotfish is another predator of the reef," Professor Garcia said. "They will nibble on the reef, and if you get very close you can actually hear them eating the reef skeleton. It does make a crunching sound. And did you know when the parrotfish poops, it is actually expelling the digested coral in the form of sand?"

"Oh, yuck," Juliana said as she scrunched up her face. "Do you mean that when we walk on the beach we are actually walking on parrotfish poop?"

"I wouldn't go as far as to say that, but then you never know, do you?"

Chapter 17

While Snail and the others had been down on the wreck, a few other boats had arrived to fish or just cruise around. One boat did slow down noticeably as it passed *The White Dove*. It went another couple of hundred yards before the captain throttled down the engine and dropped anchor. They displayed their red and white dive flag, but no one entered the water. Professor Garcia hadn't paid too much attention to it arriving, as this was a rather popular dive spot for those who had permission.

Although Garcia couldn't know it, on board that boat were six divers, two of whom, including Vega, had been part of Chang's group of thugs from the San Blas Islands failure.

Vega watched the activity aboard *The White Dove* through a set of binoculars. After the dive team returned and climbed aboard, there seemed to be a lot of excitement and laughter going on as the students gathered together on the aft deck.

"Make sure the spear guns are ready," Vega said to his men. "When they go back down, we will give them a few minutes then we go after them. Mr. Chang wants to make sure that girl and her boyfriend don't come back. I have explained who we are after, and Manuel de Costa is on that boat and will point them out. Be quick down there, and let's get out of here."

Activity on *The White Dove* had settled down, and the kids were all resting. Snail, Teri, Eamon, and Christina were still chatting about the Crown of Thorns and wanted to blow up the photograph of it.

"I bet that Crown of Thorns starfish had at least ten or twelve legs," Teri said. "It was huge."

"I'm thirsty," Snail said. "Does anyone want some water or something to eat?"

The four walked to the ice chests that had been placed in the galley, selected what they wanted, and returned to their seats. The sun was high in the early afternoon sky and the temperature was perfect. The thought of going into the wreck in a few hours was exciting, but Du-Juan's strange behavior was also on Snail's mind. He had moved himself closer to Du-Juan to keep an eye on him to see if he did anything unusual. He didn't. Du-Juan had found a vacant chair and was asleep.

Two hours later the group of divers had donned fresh tanks and were ready to re-enter the ocean for the second dive. Alonzo had given them the layout of the interior of the wreck and reminded them of the crocodile shark, as there might be others inside the wreck. He also reemphasized that if they saw a Crown of Thorns starfish, not to touch it.

"The relics on the ship remain on the ship," Professor Garcia reminded everyone, "as we are not allowed to take anything off of it."

He then asked Snail, an experienced wreck diver, to explain to the other students what they needed to know and understand about exploring inside the wreck.

"You are all experienced divers, so use your common sense," Snail said, "and don't grab or pull on anything underwater. Next, the only special pieces of equipment we will need are lanterns to light our way through the ship and a guideline, which will be secured at the entrance. Captain Alonzo will secure the line once we enter the ship and will play it out as we go through. If by some chance you become lost, stop what you are doing. Don't panic because that leads to trouble. Instead, just start banging on your tank with your dive knife. We will find you.

Now, when you enter through the capstan keep your arms close to your body unless you need them to navigate through the opening. Also keep your feet close together, so you can easily drop down to the deck below. Space will be limited inside the hull, so give your dive partner ample space, and let's have a nice uneventful dive."

The visibility had improved since the morning. Everything looked different and so beautiful. In a short five minutes they arrived at the wreck and made one quick pass over the deck before entering.

Pedro Lorino, the lookout on Vega's boat, announced that the divers had just entered the water and for his buddies to get ready.

"Let's get in," Vega said, "and get this job done as quickly as possible. I don't want to be here any longer than necessary. It's too dangerous."

Of the six men who dove, three carried spear guns and three carried knives. One of the men, Mario Nuñez, who toted a spear gun, asked, "Why does that man want these kids killed?"

"He didn't say," Roberto Vega quickly responded, "so I didn't ask, and you shouldn't either. For what he is paying us, it is best not to ask too many questions. Just do what he says."

"Why aren't you diving?" Pedro asked. "You know what they look like."

"That girl's boyfriend was the one responsible for pulling

out my front teeth, so I can't bite down on my mouthpiece. Now, enough talk, get going."

Given the clarity of the water, the divers had a great view of the wreck as they swam over. Scanning the deck for any hiding predators and not seeing any, Alonzo swam over to mid-deck where the capstan once stood. He marshaled the students and one by one they entered following exactly the way Snail had described.

Du-Juan was the last student to enter. He approached the capstan and, just as he slipped through, looked back at Manuel. But Manuel was swimming away.

He's supposed to be with us, Du-Juan thought. *Where's he going?* The young man knew something wasn't right. He had to do something.

The inside of the wreck was cramped from years of decomposition and saturation. It would be easy for someone to get injured by one of the broken planks that were obstacles.

Du-Juan was suddenly in a panic. He needed to get word to Snail that something bad was going to happen, but he couldn't navigate around the other divers to get to him. He realized what he had done was terribly wrong, and now all the students' lives were in danger.

Du-Juan moved up and grabbed Juliana's fin and gave it a tug. She stopped and spun around banging her tanks against a broken bean. She gave Du-Juan a questioning look and shrugged her shoulders. Du-Juan carefully pushed her out of his way and swam forward toward Eamon and did the same with him. Slowly he made his way up to Snail. Cautiously Du-Juan grabbed Snail's fin and gave it a tug. Snail stopped and spun around. They were face to face.

Du-Juan froze for a moment. Then knowing what he was doing was right, he reached over and took Snail's hand and with his index finger wrote a "d" in his palm, then looked up at Snail wanting to know if he understood.

Snail shook his head, not understanding.

Again Du-Juan took his finger and repeated making a "d" followed by an "a". Snail gave him a nod. Du-Juan slowly wrote "danger" on Snail's palm.

Snail frowned down at his palm, and then pointed down, inside the ship. He then pointed his finger toward the side of the boat.

Du-Juan didn't understand what Snail was trying to communicate. He was becoming desperate. He needed to convey to Snail and the others about what would happen once they left the wreck. He held up his hand and moved Snail out of the way and swam past Teri, and up to Alonzo who he knew carried an underwater writing tablet. Stopping Alonzo with a rude tug, Du-Juan grabbed the tablet and swam back to Snail.

But as Du-Juan was turning around he caught his shoulder on a ragged broken beam, which ripped through his wetsuit top and cut him deeply. He began to bleed immediately. The dinner bell for the sharks had just rung.

Ignoring the injury, Du-Juan returned to Snail who had managed to move up closer and waited. Du-Juan returned and penned, DANGER ON THE DECK. He showed the note to Snail. Next he wrote, CHANG'S MEN ARE WAITING FOR YOU.

Snail stared down at what Du-Juan had written, hardly daring to believe it. He pointed to the word CHANG. Du-Juan nodded. So it *was* Chang. He was in Panama.

Snail needed to think clearly and quickly. He grabbed the board from Du-Juan's hand and got Alonzo's attention. He pointed at the note and indicated they needed to leave the wreck the same way they came in. He figured if Du-Juan had informed Chang on their dive this afternoon, he would have most likely have told him where they would be exiting the wreck and that was where his men would be waiting.

But the first thing they needed to do was to stop the bleeding on Du-Juan's shoulder. The blood in the water had already flowed outside the wreck with the current, so they needed to move quickly. Du-Juan was not big by any means and got cold fast, so he had opted to wear the wetsuit top. This turned out to be a good thing.

Snail pulled Du-Juan closer and removed his dive knife from his belt. He cut a chunk out of Du-Juan's wetsuit top, laid it over the injury, and placed Du-Juan's hand on it to hold it in place. At least it would slow down the amount of blood seeping out.

Next he took the board and gathered all the students and Alonzo as close as he could to himself. He pointed to Du-Juan's note on the board: DANGER ON THE DECK. He showed everyone the note and waited until he received an acknowledgement. Next he wrote: STAY CLOSE TO EACH OTHER. Again he showed the note to everyone. Finally, he wrote to Du-Juan, HOW MANY?

Du-Juan shrugged his shoulders, indicating he didn't know.

He cleared the board again and wrote: OUTSIDE THE WRECK FORM A CIRCLE. He showed the note to everyone then wrote: GIRLS INSIDE GUYS OUTSIDE. Next note: MOVE AS QUICKLY AS POSSIBLE. He figured by keeping everyone close they would have a better chance of survival, sort of like security in numbers.

Taking a deep breath, Snail realigned the divers. They began making their way to the capstan entrance. That was when Snail noticed that Manuel was not inside the wreck. He made a head count and confirmed Manuel was missing. He then realized that was why the alarm went off. He knew he had seen that face before. Now he remembered when and where. He was one of the men who had attacked them during the San Blas Islands dive. That was what the bruises were; Manuel was on the receiving end of Snail's finger jab. Manuel must be part of the gang that would be attacking the students as soon as they exited the wreck.

Working in the small cramped space below the capstan

opening, Snail aligned himself with Eamon, followed by the ladies then behind them Du-Juan and Alonzo. Snail would be first out of the wreck. If he didn't see any danger he would give the okay signal. Snail took his place by the opening, gave one more look back at his friends, and then ascended.

He stuck his head out of the opening expecting to be immediately attacked but saw no one. Temporarily relieved, he urged the others to hurry up and pushed himself clear. Each diver moved out smartly until Juliana got her BC snagged on a broken beam, ripping a hole in it. Her BC was now useless as it would not be able to hold any air. Behind her Alonzo saw what happened and was able to get her free.

Snail had kept an eye open for Manuel and his friends. As of this moment, none were visible. The group moved as quickly as they could away from the wreck. Almost immediately they were met by ten circling hammerhead sharks. Snail looked over at Du-Juan and noticed blood was again seeping from his wetsuit vest. At this time, that was the worst thing that could happen. Sharks have thousands of sensors all along their snouts and head picking up on sounds of distress and the smell of blood. Eamon also saw this and moved over to Du-Juan to apply pressure against the wound, trying to stem the flow of blood.

Snail pointed to the sharks and instantly his mind flashed back to Catalina Island many years ago when a great Mako shark attacked his father. Carmine had barely survived the attack by relying on his wit, knowledge, and courage. Snail quickly pulled out his dive knife for that one small piece of protection, even knowing it would never penetrate the thick rough skin of a shark.

The sharks came close a couple of times, heading mainly toward the smell of blood. One did bump into Du-Juan but kept swimming. The first couple of minutes, swimming to the surface went fine with no intruders other than the sharks, but then Snail heard the bang of a dive knife against a scuba tank. Snail spun around, looking for who was sending out the signal when he spotted Eamon. He was pointing at a group of divers, approaching them over the wreck. Then off to the left of the group, Snail spotted a lone diver and assumed it was Manuel. He pointed toward the single diver, who headed toward the approaching divers but then suddenly veered toward the kids. He was moving fast.

Snail's eyes followed the lone diver and decided it would be best to intercept him before he did harm to the student divers. Off like a rocket, Snail closed the distance. They reached each other about midway between the students and the other group of men. Snail could see that Manuel had hate in his eyes as he surged upward through the water. Snail wasn't going to be done in by Manuel and decided to take the fight to him.

With about five yards separating the two, Manuel paused, took aim, and fired his spear gun at Snail. But Snail had already decided what he was going to do. As soon as the spear gun fired, Snail stopped swimming and placed his body at an angle away from the shot. It missed by barely a foot.

Seeing that Manuel didn't have any extra spear shafts with him to reload his gun, Snail charged the shooter. He grabbed the spear launcher. But Manual was suddenly jolted from behind. He slumped in Snail's arms, and blood started to circle the two divers.

Looking over Manuel's shoulder, Snail could see a spear shaft lodged in his back. He had been shot by one of the other attackers. This was the second dinner bell for the sharks. Snail didn't like the predicament he was in and needed to move swiftly.

Snail had two choices. He could leave Manuel for the sharks or he could try to take him back and hope he survived to be turned him over to the authorities. He knew he couldn't just leave Manuel for the sharks, so he hoped for the best.

Holding on to Manuel as tightly as he could, Snail pumped his flippers and tried to follow his group as they continued to ascend. Alonzo was still in charge, leading them topside. Looking back down at Snail with the injured man, Eamon hand-gestured to the others to keep going, and then turned and swam down to help Snail.

By the time Eamon and Snail had joined up, two of the other attackers with spear guns had closed enough for one of them to take a shot. It missed both boys but hit Manuel again close to previous spear. More blood meant more sharks. Panic time for everyone underwater! The two attackers began swimming directly toward the two young men.

Eamon and Snail saw the two heading directly for them, glanced at each other, and realized they had to release their grip on Manuel if they were going to survive. Snail let go first, holding up his hand. Eamon followed and watched as Manuel's body slowly drifted downward, leaving a trail of blood as it descended. The boys kept a close eye on the sharks, as they appeared to be heading toward Manuel. It was a horrible thought knowing they possibly could have saved him but they had to save themselves.

Snail and Eamon went after the attackers with a vengeance. The two intruders were no match for the young men who out-muscled them from the beginning. Without hesitating, Snail grabbed the first man by the facemask and ripped it off, then poked him in the eye, temporarily blinding him. He didn't know which way to go—he had lost sight of both Snail and the sharks. Eamon followed Snail into the attack and tried to copy the move, but it didn't work. The second diver spun around and began heading for the boat as fast as he could.

The sharks didn't approach the boys, but instead were closing in on the retreating attackers, now in the vast cloud of blood from Manuel's wounds. The sight wasn't pretty. Piercing screams could be heard as the sharks attacked the divers. Snail and Eamon did all they could not to look and headed toward the surface to rejoin the others.

Teri and the group of divers broke the surface above Snail and Eamon after their long three-minute decompression stop. Everyone waited for the last two to break the surface but they hadn't.

A long couple of minutes passed before Eamon and Snail could come up but as soon as they did Eamon immediately called out saying they were all right.

When Snail and Eamon were aboard, they told everyone what happened.

"We had to make a decision about Manuel," Snail gasped. "If we had held on to him then we would have been in danger with the sharks and the men attacking us. So we released him and watched as he slipped deeper in the water, some of the sharks followed his blood trail. I don't know if he was alive or not, but at that moment, it really wasn't that important. Getting back here was."

"What happened to the other men, Snail?" asked Professor Garcia.

"Eamon and I went after them, had a little struggle, then they took off. I believe they drew the sharks' attention with all their swimming. The sharks followed them and, well, the rest isn't very pretty. We took the opportunity to get out while the sharks were on an eating frenzy."

On the other boat, Vega waited impatiently for his divers to return. He did not know they had been the sharks' main course just a short time ago, but he would wait until Alonzo pulled up anchor and left. Only then would he leave.

Chapter 18

It took the Coast Guard nearly an hour to arrive. When they did it was as if they were making an invasion on a terrorist ship. The accompanying Marine detachment boarded *The White Dove* with their weapons drawn, ready for a fight. Their yelling and screaming put everyone in a state of fear. It took both Alonzo and Professor Garcia some time before they convinced the invading Marines of what actually happened.

"The way the Marines acted is not unusual," said Alonzo through Professor Garcia. "There are a lot of illegal drugs coming in from South America and Mexico these days, and everyone is on edge. The damage they do to people's lives is incredible."

Then the questions began, fast and furious. Marine Captain Del Gatto, in charge of the detachment that boarded *The White Dove,* conducted what felt like an interrogation.

"We have to be prepared when we board and commandeer crafts suspected of carrying drugs or other contraband into Panama." He was the one who asked the questions. If he didn't like the answer he kept asking the same question over and over until he received the answer he was looking for. Professor Garcia had to intervene a few times to get the Marine captain to understand that it was they who were attacked and not the other way around.

Then Del Gatto stated that college students used a lot of drugs and Americans were some of the worst. It took some convincing, but the Coast Guard finally allowed them to leave after they got everyone's name, address, and contact information.

"That was completely uncalled for," Eamon said. "We didn't deserve this sort of treatment."

"Yes, you are right. When we return to the port I will call and lodge a complaint with the Coast Guard. I apologize for their behavior." Professor Garcia was quite upset by the Coast Guard's actions and was going to make sure everyone knew it.

Snail stepped forward and said he would pull up the anchor when Alonzo gave him the word. He had Garcia relay this to the captain; the captain nodded that he understood.

It had been a nerve-wracking experience, and they were all glad to be heading back to the camp. Snail wanted to get with Du-Juan and find out how Chang contacted him and what his evil nemesis's overall plans were. He was going to speak with him now, but then he noticed Juliana was really giving him the business. She was clearly upset as she waved her finger in his face. Snail decided to wait until they were back on land.

Back at the lodge and after a quick shower, Snail went to Du-Juan's room. He rapped on the door a couple of times before it was answered. It was Eamon.

"Hi Eamon, where's Du-Juan?"

"Du-Juan is here sitting on the bed," Eamon said quietly. "He's been crying all evening. Juliana tore him to shreds on the boat after she found out that he was connected to the attack, and he knows you're really angry. He's afraid of you, Snail, so use kid gloves, if you know what I mean."

"I do," Snail said, taking a deep breath. "But I plan on finding out what this is all about."

Eamon stepped back and allowed Snail to enter the room. He saw the shell of a broken young man sitting on the bed. His face was streaked with tears. Snail approached.

"I'm not going to ask you how you are because it's pretty obvious you're not very well. But you need to tell me about Chang and how you hooked up with him. And Du-Juan, I need to know the truth."

Du-Juan let out a long sigh, then began.

"Chang came to me last year when I needed money for school. I don't know how he found out, but somehow he did. He came up to me at my house and said I could earn some spending cash if I did some work for him at the university."

"Did you ask him what this work was before you accepted the money?"

"I did. He said he was writing a book about you and he wanted to know about your activities and your relationship with Teri. He said to keep it quiet and tell him when I learned anything. Your football career has been in the papers for the past couple of years so that was easy to compile and I added a few more bits of information I had heard. He seemed to be happy with that."

"What about this trip to Panama? What did you tell him, or more important, what did he ask you to do?"

"He said that I would get an extra ten thousand dollars if I did what he wanted me to do, and that was to isolate you and Teri from the group. I needed the ten grand, so I agreed. It was the other night, when he said that he wanted you and Teri to never return to the boat, when I realized his intentions were purely evil."

"Why didn't you tell me then? You could have easily come to my room and spoke with me. None of this would have happened."

"I was afraid. I was scared at what you would do to me."

"I would have done nothing to you, but I would have forewarned the other divers and prevented Professor Garcia from getting injured, and you too. I'm not a mean person. I would have respected you for telling me the truth up front."

"I know that now. I'm sorry."

"You do know that you put more than Teri and me in danger, don't you? You put every diver in peril because of your actions, and that includes Juliana. I think she likes you, or at least she liked you before all this happened."

"She's the first girl that ever showed any interest in me. I do like her, but she was right and so are you. I should have done something before so many people got hurt."

Snail was angry and fought really hard to keep his temper under control.

"Okay, Du-Juan," he said finally, "now I want you to tell me everything about Chang. What's his next move? When will we be seeing him again? What are his plans for Teri or me? I need to know everything right now."

"All I know is that he said if his men fail to stop you on the wreck, he will personally come to the farewell dinner and take care of you there."

"Did he say how he would do that?"

"No, only that you would never see it happen."

"Okay, Du-Juan, if you make contact with him before the dinner tomorrow night, then I suggest you tell me everything that is said, and I mean everything. Hold out one nugget of information and I find out, then you will be sorry."

"You do know, you and he were in the same restaurant last week."

"We were? When?"

"When we ate at the Ego y Narcisco Restaurant. He was there with another man. I forgot his name."

"Describe him to me. What does he look like?"

"You know, he isn't real tall. He has long hair, a skimpy mustache, wears sunglasses and part of left ear is missing."

"What do you mean missing?"

"Just what I said, the top of the ear is missing, like it had been bitten off."

"Bitten off?" Snail had to think about that. "Where would he have had his ear bitten off?"

"I don't know, but he said you were responsible for it." Du-Juan looked at Snail as if he knew what he was talking about.

"Okay, thanks, Du-Juan. If you can remember anything else let me know. If you speak with him, tell me everything that is said. Got that?"

"Yes, I got that."

"Go apologize to Juliana. It might make you feel better, and her too. Good night."

Snail said good evening to Eamon as he left the room. He went straight to Teri.

"Have I got some news to tell you."

The two talked about Du-Juan, Chang, and everything that had happened since the trip to San Blas Islands.

"While Du-Juan was describing what Chang looks like he said he has a missing ear. He said I was responsible for it being gone. But how in the world did he lose his ear?"

"It's not about losing his ear as much as something happened to it." Teri said, then smiled. "I know what happened to it."

"You do? Tell me."

"When Chang escaped from us last Christmas on the bayou, Bernadotte sent her panther after him. I don't think her intention was to kill Chang but just scare him. That is probably what happened. The panther stalked Chang until she was able to get him down and bite his ear off. That's the only way that I can think of that he lost his ear."

"That makes perfect sense to me. Bernadotte was a pretty impressive lady, and her panther was a really powerful animal." He paused for a moment then said, "If Chang does show up we'll be ready for him. I just hope he doesn't do something that puts everyone in danger—again." He paused a moment and looked at Teri. "I wonder if Chang was responsible for the sinking of Dad's boat? I wouldn't put it past that sneaky skunk to do something that dastardly. My gut tells me so."

Chapter 19

During the drive back to Panama City, Du-Juan stood up to get everyone's attention. With his head bowed he apologized for his role in the attack. He gave a shortened version of the story he had given to Snail the previous night. He also answered all questions thrown at him by his shocked classmates, or at least tried to.

"I am so sorry for putting everyone at risk and in harm's way," he concluded. "I really am. Professor Garcia was injured, I got my shoulder cut open, and I placed all of you in danger. I never realized just how bad Mr. Chang was until all this happened."

Du-Juan's explanation and apology seemed to be accepted. When he finished speaking, Snail, Teri, and Professor Garcia sat at the back of the bus and discussed Chang and everything

Du-Juan had said. They needed to be able to turn Chang in to the proper authorities, but how could they do that if they didn't know where he was? They didn't even know if he had anything else planned for them, possibly putting the class in danger again. So, together, they came up with a plan.

After they finished speaking, Professor Garcia called Du-Juan to come and sit with them.

"This is what you are going to do, Du-Juan," the professor said, "and make sure you follow these directions to the letter. So, when we get back to the university, you are going to call Chang and tell him where we are going this afternoon. Tell him that Teri and Snail are going to return to the Ego y Narcisco Restaurant because they enjoyed their tapas. From the restaurant Teri and Snail are going to walk back to the Cathedral to see the tower one more time. Teri said she wanted to take a few more pictures. They will be alone. Can you do that?"

Du-Juan didn't immediately respond. Instead he remained quiet.

Again, the professor asked, "Can you do what we are asking?"

"Yes, I think so."

"No, not think so. You either do it or not." Garcia's voice was firm.

After a very long pause Du-Juan finally answered, "Yes, I will do it. But let me say I won't be responsible if anything happens to either Snail or Teri."

"Du-Juan, you just make the phone call. Let me worry about everything else," Snail said.

Back in their seats Snail leaned very close to Teri and whispered, "I still don't trust him."

"Why? He's agreed to co-operate."

"He knows more than what he's saying. I don't buy his story. I don't know why, I can't put my finger on it, but I still don't trust him." Holding both of Teri's hands, he said, "Are you sure you are up for this? I would be devastated if anything bad happened to you."

"That's sweet of you to say, but we're in this together. Now, let's just relax and see what happens this afternoon."

As soon as the bus parked and the bags were unloaded, Du-Juan made a beeline to his room to supposedly make his call. Snail watched him as he darted off, hoping he would do it as he was instructed. Looking for Eamon, Snail walked over to him.

"Eamon, keep an eye on him for me. My gut isn't a hundred percent convinced he's being honest. Can you do this, please?"

"Absolutely." Eamon picked up his backpack and headed toward his room.

Two hours later, after showers and a change of clothes, Teri and Snail headed off for tapas at the Ego y Narcisco restaurant. Dressed in clean shorts, UCLA T-shirts, and running shoes, they were prepared to make a quick get away if necessary. Neither one was particularly hungry, but they needed to go through the motions of their plan if they were going to stop Chang once and for all.

They were seated near the back of the restaurant so they

could keep an eye on everyone entering the restaurant. A few early afternoon diners came in, but no one looked like Chang. One man did come in and sat two tables away from the kids, but paid them no attention. He sat quietly and ordered his meal, ate his tapas, then ordered a second helping. They didn't think too much about him.

While they waited for Chang to appear they nibbled on shrimp and mango in a pineapple sauce and grilled eggplant. The food was great but they didn't have an appetite to appreciate it. Still no Chang.

"Okay, Teri," Snail said finally, "it doesn't appear as if Mr. Chang is going to come. Let's head over to the tower and see if he shows up there. I just hope Du-Juan made that phone call."

Snail asked directions on how to get to the tower from where they were now. He was given directions, paid for their meal, and escorted Teri out the door.

"Snail," Teri asked as they stepped out onto the street, "you know how to get to the cathedral from here—why did you ask?"

"I did in case that man sitting close to us needed to know. Maybe he is with Chang. Just a gut feeling."

The warmth of the afternoon was pleasant, but the humidity was high. Snail began sweating. He claimed it was the heat, but in reality he was nervous about what might happen very shortly.

As soon as they left, the man sitting near them pulled out his cellular phone and made a call. When he finished he tossed down money for his meal then quickly left the Ego y Narcisco.

He spotted Snail right off, as he was taller and certainly larger than most locals. Teri was beside him holding his hand. The walk to the tower was about a mile and there was only one way to get there. The man tucked himself into an alley and waited for Vega, as instructed.

The restaurant was at the edge of town, and Snail and Teri had to pass a commercial area with buildings and alleyways before they picked up the main road leading to the tower. Snail anticipated that if something were going to happen, this would be the best location. He didn't know where or when, but figured if one or two guys came after them he could easily take charge of the situation.

"Snail, I'm sorry that we didn't see Chang today. I honestly thought he would show up at the restaurant."

"Well we may not have seen him at the restaurant, but I think he will make an appearance. I can almost guarantee it."

They walked on in silence for a few more minutes when the sounds of a car rapidly accelerating in their direction caught their attention. Snail paused and looked over his shoulder and saw an old beat up Ford racing toward them. It pulled up with a screech of tires, and three men leaped out.

"Time to move, babe."

He took her hand, and they darted off down the road to the first alleyway they came to, turned, and ran down it and stopped. It was a dead end. Snail made sure Teri was protected, then stuck his head up and waited for the men to approach.

The three attackers turned the corner leading into the alleyway, slowing to a walk as they searched. Snail watched as they stopped and looked around.

"Listen for them," one of them ordered the others. "There is no place for them to go. You two walk down the left side, and I'll take the right. Look under, over, and inside every box, trashcan, and container. They have to be here, somewhere."

Snail quickly noted that the apparent leader of the group was walking down his side of the alleyway by himself. The others were on the other side of the alley. This was good.

The thugs were anything but quiet as they tossed boxes and trashcans about the alleyway, searching for their prey. They yelled and screamed as stray dogs, cats, and a few rats fled the noise. The three men had moved about halfway down the alley when the thug on the right suddenly went flying across the alley and crashed into some partially filled trashcans. He landed with a thud, bounced once, and lay still. The other men, who were walking just ahead of him, spun around at the noise.

"Mario," one of them shouted, "what happened?"

"Mario isn't going to answer you," came a voice from where Mario had been.

It was Eamon's voice. Snail appeared from behind the box he'd been using as cover, staring at his friend. Eamon grinned at him.

"Hi, Snail."

"Where did you come from?"

"We followed you from the restaurant. We didn't want you to have all the fun by yourself … and we were a little concerned."

"Who are we?"

"Professor Garcia, Christina, Juliana, and the police." Eamon looked over to the attackers and asked, "Where's Chang?"

Neither thug said a word for a few seconds. Then one slapped his buddy on the shoulder, and together they charged Snail and Eamon. Big mistake.

Snail grabbed a trashcan and with all his strength threw it at the two advancing men, striking one dead center in the chest. He went down in a heap. The second saw this, skidded to a stop, and suddenly decided it would be best to exit the area real fast. He turned and ran back down the alley. Snail was on his trail in a flash.

The thug was nearing the entrance of the alley when two police officers stepped out and blocked him. He slid to a stop. Not wanting to get caught by the police, he turned and saw Snail approaching fast. He just couldn't react fast enough. Snail smashed into him like a football-tackling dummy, and they both went down in a pile with Snail being on top.

The wind had been knocked from the man's lungs, and he was hurting. That didn't stop Snail. He reached down, grabbed the man by the shirt, and pulled him to his feet, actually pulled him off his feet and high into the air. Snail was angry. He had a strong grip on the man's shirt and while still in the air banged him against the wall of the closest building with a horrendous thud.

It was all over in a few seconds. Snail was surprised to see Professor Garcia, with his arm still in a sling with Teri and Eamon leading the first thug down the alley toward Snail. Juliana and Christina were carrying the second thug. Two other police officers followed behind them. He had expected to see the police—that was part of the plan—but not the others.

"I didn't know you were planning on coming along, Professor?"

"I did. I thought the added insurance of a few extra bodies was necessary just in case the situation got nasty."

Before they left the scene, Garcia asked the men where Chang was hiding. They said they didn't know. All they knew was a friend had called and offered them the chance to make some money to do a simple job. That's it.

Professor Garcia didn't believe them, but he didn't want to waste any more time questioning them. He told the police if they got any information on Chang or if someone bailed them out of jail, he wanted to know immediately. He provided the police with a cell phone number and they left.

"Snail, Teri, would you still like to take that one last walk to the tower today?"

"Professor, you mentioned the other day about a hidden treasure, one that belonged to the locals when Morgan invaded. Do you mind if we have a look to see if there is one?" Eamon asked.

"I can assure you, if there was one it has either been found long ago or is so well-hidden it will never be uncovered. But to satisfy your curiosity, sure, I'll talk to the rangers and see if we can have one look around the area. You never know what you may find."

Chapter 20

Not too far away from the students, a couple of men stood by watching their every move. One of the men, Jorge, was from the restaurant, and the other was Roberto Vega. Vega had been with Chang when the call came in and was immediately dispatched to help out.

Together they watched as the three groups of students broke up and went separate ways.

"Jorge," Vega growled, "you know Chang is upset with what's happened. He told me to stick with you and watch these kids. If there is a treasure, Chang wants it. He said he will pay us well when we turn it over to him."

"Roberto, Chang is insane. He wants those kids hurt and for what reason? He never said. Now he wants us to take this treasure that may not even exist and give it to him. Has he paid you yet for what you've done? I haven't seen any money."

"He has the money, I've seen it. He won't pay out until the deed is done. Now, let's just watch and wait for those kids to find what they are searching for and then we will take it. Do you have your gun?"

"Yes, but I don't want to use it."

"Okay, give it to me. I'm not afraid to do so." Vega held out his hand and waited for Jorge to give up his weapon. He reluctantly handed it over.

"I hope you know what you are getting yourself into, because I certainly don't." Jorge quit speaking to Vega and directed his attention toward the professor and his students.

The idea of searching for a lost treasure energized the students. Everyone was sure they would find it. If a treasure was found, they would turn it over to the Church and they could use it for charity.   While Professor Garcia spoke with one of the rangers on the night shift, the students discussed their best plan of action.

"Snail," Eamon asked, "If you were a priest, where would you hide the treasure?"

"I'm not sure. Maybe in the graveyard. From what I've read, many people didn't like to venture into the area of the dead. That to me would be a good place to start."

"If I was a priest," Teri said, "that's where I would bury

it. But since I would be a nun, I think I would hide it in the floor of the cathedral, probably in a cubby hole beneath a rug or table or even under the alter."

"Or remove a brick from one of the open areas like a window and hide it in there," Christina said.

"Those are all good ideas, but let me suggest something before we get started," the professor said.

"What's that?" Juliana asked.

"I have been to these ruins many times, and I know the area quite well. The graveyard you are speaking about is not that close to the cathedral, and people looking for artifacts inside the graves have ransacked it many times over the years. It is a shame what damage has been done to the graves. So, to be honest with you, even the smallest hidden treasure in the graveyard would have been discovered.

"Now, with that said, I believe the ladies have made an interesting point. The nuns could have been in possession of the items given by the villagers, and they may have hidden them somewhere in the cathedral."

"But the cathedral is nearly all ruins now. There are no floors, no doors, no rugs or even any furniture," Eamon said as he looked at the old structure.

"That is true. The building has nearly been destroyed over the centuries. If there were a treasure stashed somewhere other than the lower floor, then it most likely would have been found. But none has been found, and I believe the girls may be right."

"So what are you suggesting, Professor?" Snail asked.

"I am suggesting that we start at the ground floor and have

a close look at it. Between the rubble and the snakes that may be living inside, it is not one hundred percent safe, so we would be best to search during the day. And just in case, we could probably use a ladder and flashlights.

"This is what I recommend. It is late and we need to get back to the dormitory. I will make arrangements for ladders and flashlights to be here in the morning; we can start our search tomorrow. Is that alright with everyone?"

He was met with enthusiastic approval.

Jorge and Roberto watched as the professor and the kids headed back toward the university. The professor had spent some time talking to the rangers, and when they left they were talking about getting flashlights, ladders, and other tools to 'help them with their find'.

Vega clapped Jorge on the shoulder. "See? They know something. Let's go have a look around. If we take care of these kids, and find the treasure, that'll be sure to make Chang happy."

Waiting until everyone had left, the two thugs moved toward the cathedral and entered the old structure.

"There is nothing here," Jorge said nervously. "These kids are imagining things if they think there is a treasure buried in the cathedral."

"There is nothing to worry about. Let's look around for a few minutes then we will leave. Besides, it's getting dark, and we don't have a flashlight."

Tripping and stumbling over the debris put Jorge in a foul mood. He wanted to leave right now, but Vega was not having it. Jorge continued to argue, saying one more fall and he was gone. Almost as soon as he said it, Jorge stumbled again with a loud clatter of stones. Vega laughed but quit laughing when he heard Jorge scream out.

"What's wrong with you?"

Jorge didn't say a word. He stood up and hanging from his arm was a four-foot bushmaster snake. "Help me, Vega."

Vega's blood froze as he looked at Jorge, knowing he could do nothing for the man. He stared at him for many seconds, trembling in fear before he ran, leaving Jorge to die alone.

Vega didn't go back to Mr. Chang's room. Instead, he hid out for a while, remembering the pleading look on Jorge's face as the man struggled for life. After he calmed down, Vega called Chang and informed him of what happened.

"Did you find anything?" Chang demanded.

"No, only the snake."

"This is what is going to happen. Tomorrow night there is a farewell dinner for the students. We will be there. Vega, you and I are going to be waiters for an evening. After tomorrow, I will be rid of those meddling kids. Be here at 6:00 p.m. and don't be late."

Vega stood trembling at Chang's words. He had no desire to be put in harm's way anymore by a man he knew was insane. Vega took a deep breath and made the decision that enough is enough. *Chang, you can do whatever you want, I am leaving* here and be just like Captain Salazar, I am going to disappear and you will never find me.

Chapter 21

Their last full day in Panama was filled with potential. Snail got up early and woke his friends, eager to look for the treasure. Most of the other students slept in, or had plans for shopping or the beach. They were not very interested in a treasure hunt, having had enough excitement for one trip.

Down in the dining hall, Snail and Eamon picked up four cups of coffee, one each for themselves and their girlfriends. They were excited. They felt that a treasure was close at hand, and they would find it. Snail looked at his watch and told the girls to hurry up because the professor would be downstairs in ten minutes.

Just as they left the room, Juliana emerged from her room, ready for the dig.

"Let's go and have some fun," she said when the group was

assembled. "I feel it in my bones that today is the day."

"Hear, hear," Eamon said enthusiastically.

Down in the lobby Professor Garcia was waiting. Snail spotted him and yelled out, "*Buenos Dias, señor.*"

"*Buenos Dias.* Are you all ready?"

"Yes, let's do it," Eamon said.

"I have called ahead this morning and the groundskeeper will have ladders and a shovel for our use."

They strolled down the walkway to the van and within minutes were on their way. Teri was quiet this morning, thinking about the items the poor peasants had left with the priest so Morgan couldn't get his hands on it.

"I hope we find that treasure, Snail," she whispered.

Professor Garcia stood up and addressed the group.

"When we get to the cathedral, we need to find a safe place to stand the ladders. I recommend that we give the floor a good going over. I personally think whatever treasure is here, if there even is a treasure, would be in the floor, not necessarily in a wall."

"Why would you say that?" Juliana asked.

"Well, I've been thinking of that. If I were an invader, where would I be looking for items? The first thing I would do would be to look at the walls, ceiling, behind pictures, and lastly under furniture. By then the amount of rubble on the floor would be significant, so conducting the thorough search would be more difficult. I am hoping that is what happened."

"That makes sense to me," Juliana said.

As they approached the cathedral, the bus driver said there

were some police cars and an ambulance parked. Professor Garcia asked the driver to stop so he could go see what the problem was. The professor hopped out and strolled over to speak with a police sergeant.

"The priest found a dead man inside the cathedral this morning," the sergeant advised. "He had been bitten by a snake. There were two snakes, when we arrived. One got away but one remained there so we had to kill it before we could get to the body. Who are you, sir?"

"I am Professor Garcia, from the University of Panama, and I have some students from the US who are here to look at the cathedral. I have made arrangements with the Monsignor and he has given us his approval. Is the man who died still here? Do you know who he is?"

"Yes, he is here, but he had no identification on him. Here he comes now." The Panamanian EMTs had the victim on a gurney and were having difficulty getting it over the rocky entrance.

Snail and Eamon hopped off the bus to see what was happening.

"What's up, Doc?" Snail said with a sudden smile. "I've always wanted to say that."

"Apparently there was a man in the cathedral last night who got bitten by a snake. He has died. Why don't you two go see if you can help the EMTs?"

"Come on, Eamon, let's go help."

The two ran up to the EMTs and just as they got there to assist, the gurney tipped over and the victim fell to the ground.

Everyone froze at the sight.

Snail looked at the man's face in astonishment.

"I've seen that man's face before. Professor, this is the man who was sitting next to us yesterday at the restaurant while we were waiting for Chang to show up."

Garcia and the sergeant walked over to Snail.

"The man didn't pay any attention to us," Snail added. "He just sat there eating."

While the EMTs put the victim back on the gurney, the sergeant asked a few more questions, then collected his men and they left the cathedral.

"That's the only excitement I want today," Professor Garcia said, "except for finding the treasure. Let's get started."

He waved for the rest of the group to join them. Once together, he reminded the kids about the snakes.

It didn't take the students long to start searching once they had broken into their respective groups. This time they each carried a stick to probe the crevices created by the rubble to make sure that if there were snakes hiding; they would come out and hopefully scurry off without harming anyone.

Carefully they moved about the interior of the cathedral. Snail and Eamon set up one ladder while Professor Garcia and Juliana placed the second. They began looking at the spots where a treasure might be hidden in the wall. The first hour was uneventful as no one saw any snakes or identified any location that appeared to be a potential hiding place. Then everyone stopped in their tracks as Christina yelled out. She leaped back stumbling over the debris.

"What's the matter, Christina?" Eamon asked. "Are you all right?"

"S… S… Snake." She squeaked out as she stared at a four-foot long bushmaster coming out of a crevice. Its head was moving back and forth; its forked tongue danced from its mouth. It looked like the snake was searching for the person who had poked a stick in its resting place and it did not look happy.

Grasping the shovel like a baseball bat, Garcia inched his way closer to the snake and swung the shovel like Babe Ruth but with only one arm. Garcia was surprisingly strong and as the blade stuck the snake it severed its head. The body immediately started coiling up, twisting around itself as it slowly died.

"Be careful of its head—the venom in its mouth is still potent." The professor moved closer and thrust the shovel under the head, picking it up so he could move it to a safe location.

"Wow, that was close," Eamon said as he stepped down from the ladder and moved close to Christina. She was shaking from fright.

"Thanks, Professor," she said, wrapping herself in Eamon's arms. That was some fast thinking on your part."

"No problem."

"I believe there is something in that crevice, though," she said. "It looked like an old burlap bag. I'm not sure."

"Show me exactly where you were poking when you saw the bag," Professor Garcia asked.

"Right over here."

It took some effort to regain her composure before she stepped back near to where the snake's body lay, but her excitement was starting to grow again.

"Just right here," she pointed. There was some recently overturned rubble near the crevice.

Eamon moved over and poked his stick under the debris.

"I hear snakes travel in pairs, so I just want to make sure this mate's friend isn't around. Maybe the one the police killed was its mate. I hope so."

He poked a few times and didn't rouse any unwanted guests. He tried to pick up the stone that rested over the spot Christina pointed out. It was way too heavy for one person to move, and he asked Snail to help.

Even with Snail's strength, the stone was too heavy.

"We need everyone over here to help us," Snail said as he drew in a big breath of air from exerting himself.

While they waited for Juliana and Teri to come down from the ladder, Snail and Eamon were able to move a few of the smaller stones, making it easier to attack the larger stone. Eamon bent down and looked under the stone to see if he could spot the bag Christina mentioned. At first he didn't see anything and asked her where exactly she'd seen the bag. She replied that it was on the left side of the stone and only a small portion of it was showing. Eamon directed his flashlight in that direction, slowly searching for the bag.

"I see it. I see an edge of what does look like a burlap bag. It looks pretty old. Snail, come here and take a look."

Snail leaned over to see what they were talking about. He tried to reach in with his arm but it was too far out of reach.

Snail figured that together, all five students should be able to move the stone enough to reach the bag without having to remove the stone completely.

"Once we get the stone high enough, Professor Garcia will be able to reach in and retrieve the bag. You guys ready?"

Taking their positions around the stone, each of them got the best handhold they could and on the count of three they lifted. The four of them struggled with the weight of the stone. Unfortunately it moved only a few inches.

"Wow, this thing is heavy," Juliana said.

"Go ahead Christina, count again." Eamon said.

"Okay, one, two, three, lift." Again the five lifted with all their might and this time the stone moved nearly a foot into the air. It was heavy and they all had to strain to keep it in the air.

"Hurry, Professor, see if you can get that bag," Snail called out. Garcia was already on his hands and knees reaching for bag. He grabbed it, but it was stuck under another stone. He withdrew and told them about a smaller stone beneath the larger one.

"Okay, I know what to do," Snail said. "This time when we lift, Eamon and I will get under the stone like we are going to do an overhead press and push from the bottom of the stone upward and to the right. Then we should be able to get the other stone. Ready?"

They repositioned themselves and prepared to lift.

"One, two, three, lift!"

With grunts and groans the five lifted the huge stone up and as soon as it was high enough Snail and Eamon quickly repositioned themselves beneath it and pushed using the strength in their legs. The stone resisted at first, but the pressure of the men pushing overcame the resistance, and the stone lifted. As quickly as they could, the girls began pushing the stone to the right, and finally the monstrous rock came around and landed away from the bag. It hit the ground with a loud crunching sound as smaller stones were crushed beneath its weight. They were then able to excavate the smaller stone that lay on top of the bag.

Everyone stopped and looked at the bag. Yes it was an old bag, probably burlap, but it was filthy and torn up so it was hard to tell.

"I just hope that this bag contains what we are searching for," Christina said as she hugged Eamon's arm.

"Christina, you found it," Teri said. "You should be the one to pick it up."

She stepped over to the bag and cleared away some of the dirt that was covering it. As soon as she tried to lift it, though, it fell apart in her hands and the contents spilled to the ground. Lying on the dirty floor was a collection of golden crosses, some with the image of Jesus, others without. She bent down and collected them, eight in all. She looked up at her companions. With tears in her eyes, she said they had found one of the treasures Morgan failed to get his hands on.

Professor Garcia left to get the Monsignor, leaving the students to continue studying the crosses.

When Garcia returned, he was with Monsignor De La Bianchi who said a silent prayer over the recovered items. He thanked each student with a warm handshake and thankful smile.

Before Monsignor De La Bianchi collected the crosses, Teri and Christina asked that they be allowed to photograph the find. He agreed. They all positioned themselves around the crosses and the Monsignor took the first picture, then Professor Garcia took one with the Monsignor. Everyone was happy and melancholy at the same time. They had made a wonderful discovery and the satisfaction that they uncovered the crucifixes, which would hopefully go to a good cause, but they were also saddened because the adventure was over. They had discovered the crosses and there was nothing left to uncover.

When the photos were done, Monsignor De La Bianchi gathered everything up to include the old bag and slowly walked back to the rectory. Professor Garcia said that the press would eventually make their way to the university to interview everyone who made the discovery.

"So be ready for an onslaught of questions," He said with a grin.

All Snail could say was that he wanted to get back to the dormitory, shower, and go the beach for a couple of hours and just relax.

The boys let the girls rest a bit before they started banging on their door, rousting them, telling them it was time for some fun in the sun.

"Meet us in the cafeteria in ten minutes," Eamon called out.

It took the girls nearly half an hour as they were in absolutely no hurry.

There were a few students sitting around the cafeteria. Word of the treasure had already spread, and there was exited chatter. Across the room sat Du-Juan and Juliana. They were talking and seemed okay, although he didn't look great. He was still stressed out over what he had done but was glad that at least Juliana was no longer mad at him. They had spoken briefly the night before, and this morning he was telling her the whole story. She was glad that he was opening up to her.

When they arrived at the beach, Teri and Christina were in their new bikinis, which they had bought on San Blas Island.

"Snail," Eamon whispered, "we are two lucky blokes."

Nothing else needed to be said.

Mr. Chang had come to the end of his rope. He had lost all faith in the men he hired to get Teri and Snail. They had all failed, and failed miserably. Even Vega couldn't do anything right. He needed to find one man whom he could trust and depend on if he was to succeed. Chang was desperate. But he knew where he could go and find that one person.

Every city has its dark side, the side of town where men and women of questionable character live, drink, fight, and do what they want. Even Chang was scared as he entered a dimly lit bar, but he showed no fear. The place reeked of cigarette smoke and other smells he couldn't identify.

The few customers looked at him when he entered. Their eyes followed his every move. Chang walked up to the bar and asked the bartender to point out a man who had courage, was mean as a snake, and who would follow directions and not ask questions.

The bartender pointed to a fairly large man, with short cropped jet-black hair and a scarred face. Chang approached the man, sat down, and placed a stack of Balboas on the table. "Do you want to earn this money?"

The man looked at the money then over to Chang before he responded with a nod.

"*Bueno,* be at the rear service entrance of the Bristol Hotel at six this evening, and be showered. I have a simple job that I need you to do. It won't take but a few minutes, and I don't want you asking me any questions. I will tell you everything you need to know when the time comes this evening. Will you do it? Will you be there at six this evening?"

The man leaned forward in his chair and stared at Chang for a long time before he reached over and took the money and pocketed it. He nodded again.

Smiling, Chang got up and left the bar.

The lady sitting next to the man asked, "Jaime, what did he want?"

"I don't know. I don't speak English." Jaime stood up and motioned for the lady to follow. "Come on, let's enjoy this man's money."

That night Snail told Teri that he felt strongly that Chang would try something. He would make one more attempt. "If Chang does show up and puts us—you—in danger, then we should have something planned. If I put my arms straight down to my sides like I'm standing at attention, looking as if I am going to do nothing, that's your signal to drop immediately to the floor and cover your head. Got that?"

"Got it. Do you really think he will try something?"

"I do, because he's already tried three times and failed. He is desperate and will go to any length to succeed. We both know that. Right?"

"Right. But, Snail, I hope you're wrong. I want this night to be memorable. This is our last night in Panama, and I want it to be fun."

"I know, so do I. But, just in case … if I want you to run, I'll lower my head, slowly, like this."

"Okay. And if I see something dangerous, and I want you to stay back, I'll hold my fists clenched at my sides."

"Deal."

Chapter 22

On their last evening in the capital city, the students from UCLA were headed for a semi-formal evening of dinner, dancing, and looking at the night-lights that showcased the Bridge of the Americas from a luxurious hotel on the waterfront. When they arrived, at each student's chair they found a gift—a beautifully handcrafted carving of one of the indigenous animals to the Darién region. There were lizards, sloths, and snakes.

Also dining with the class tonight were Professor Diego Garcia and his wife Gabriella. But the honored guests were a few of the Darién natives, friends and family of Professor Garcia. They were dressed in their finest traditional attire. Seated next to the professor was the chief of the Jivaro Indians, his wife, and half a dozen warriors and their wives.

The chief wore his warrior garb with a head covering. The

tattoos on their arms and chest depicted a religious period of time, according to their custom. The ladies wore skirts of reds, blues, and yellows that hung just below their knees. They wore white blouses with various mola designs. They also wore exquisite beaded necklaces and they all sported nose rings and earrings. Standing next to Snail, Teri, Eamon, and Christina, they looked so small. Professor Garcia and the chief were blood brothers and long-time friends.

It seemed the professor was well liked by the local community. While he was a student at UCLA he had been an All-American soccer player, but he turned down a professional contract just so he could return to Panama and teach. Now he coached soccer to young students living in the barrios, the poor area of Panama City. Many of those present knew Professor Garcia and spoke highly of him.

Near the end of the evening, after dinner had concluded, the lights were dimmed and the students began dancing. The sight that was the funniest was when Christina boldly asked the Chief if he would dance with her. To everyone's surprise he accepted. He stood and escorted her the dance floor. A gigantic smile crossed his face as he stood next to her. He had to look up to see her face, as she was a foot taller than he was. He seemed to enjoy it as he twirled her around gaily.

Chang, dressed like a waiter, arrived at their table and began clearing dishes. Since both the man Chang had hired and Vega had not showed up as ordered, Chang had had to think fast. He had put gray streaks in his hair and wore horn-rimmed glasses, making it difficult for the kids to recognize him. Teri was chatting with Christina when Chang bumped into her and dropped a plate on her lap, soiling her dress.

"You apologize for making me drop the dishes," Chang demanded.

He immediately realized the mistake his temper had caused, as Teri's eyes snapped up to stare at him.

Teri's eyes fixed on Chang when he spoke. Looking at him for the first time, she didn't immediately recognize Chang as he wore glasses, had let his hair grow long, and he wore a padded waiter's jacket that gave him the appearance he was much larger than he really was. But when he spoke again, she clearly recognized the voice.

"Snail!" she cried out.

Snail was close by speaking with Eamon.

Chang grabbed hold of Teri's arm and at the same time snatched a knife from the table, holding it to her throat.

"This girl and her boyfriend were responsible for me not getting my deserved millions of dollars from my ancestor Ching Shih's treasure."

"That's a lie." Snail yelled back. "You were trying to get your hands on illegal drugs to sell. That's where your money was going to come from. We stopped you in Hawaii, and again in Ocracoke Island. We will stop you again, Chang."

Professor Garcia translated as quickly as Snail spoke. His wife and friends looked shocked as Chang continuously threatened Teri with the knife.

While Chang struggled to hold on to Teri, his hair fell away from his head exposing his ear. That was when Teri saw the half eaten, ragged ear.

Twisting her the arm, Chang moved with her to the balcony where he threatened to throw her into the river below. "I will let the fishes eat her and you can do nothing about it."

Teri struggled, but the little man was surprisingly strong. Desperately, she looked to Snail.

He gave her their warning sign, dropping his hands down to his side. She fell to the floor and covered her head with her arms. Chang was shocked by the movement and momentarily looked down at her, taking his eyes off Snail. Snail grabbed a chair from the nearby table and hurled it with all his might at Chang. It found its mark, striking him dead center of the chest. The force was so strong that Chang dropped the knife and was flung back against the balcony railing, knocking him over it and into the rushing river below. He screamed all the way down the twenty-five foot fall.

Teri climbed to her feet, welcoming Snail's strong arms around her.

As Snail told everyone the story of Chang, the native chief motioned for two of his men to go after Chang—he simply looked at his men, nodded his head, and pointed his finger. In a flash they responded.

Chapter 23

It took the Darién Indians almost no time to locate Chang and put him on their boat, which had brought them to the dinner. He was calling out for help while struggling to get to shore. They rescued him, but instead of turning him over to the police or returning him to the restaurant, they began paddling upstream away from the hotel and civilization.

Chang tried a couple of times to escape, but the natives weren't going to allow that to happen. He was going to be their guest and that was that.

Chang didn't know where he was being taken, but he suspected nothing good was going to come of this trip. The two natives continued to paddle their canoe for over four hours, following the meandering route of the river as they headed deeper and deeper into the jungle. They navigated by the stars and landmarks along the river and eventually arrived at their destination. It was pitch black as no stars or moonlight could break through the thick overhanging foliage.

Chang was removed from the canoe, tied up and placed in a small hut. He trembled in fear for his life but still maintained his arrogant and obnoxious attitude. He continued to be verbally threatening and accusatory toward the natives, but they seemed to be immune to his noise. They didn't understand him.

Very early the next morning, before the sun rose, Chang saw the chief of the Jivaro tribe and Professor Garcia arrived at the village. The chief and professor sat by themselves for some time before the chief summoned some of his warriors and gave them instructions. Chang didn't realize it, but he was about to become the main attraction for the day. The chief sat on his throne with Garcia standing next to him. Looking at his warriors, he announced that he wanted Chang to be brought to him immediately. The same two warriors who had brought Chang to the village hurried off at their leader's command.

Chang now stood in front of the Chief and all the village elders. The chief used Professor Garcia to translate.

"Your actions last night were dangerous. Last night you threatened a young lady. You are responsible for many deaths. Now you will have to pay for your evil deeds."

Chang didn't like the sound of that.

"This is what is going to happen," The chief continued. "You are going to be given a knife and a spear and sent out into the jungle. If you encounter a wild animal you must kill it. If you encounter a warrior you must kill that warrior. If you succeed in killing the warrior, and you to make it to safety, then you are free to go. But if you fail to kill the warrior and are captured then you will be sacrificed."

Without allowing Chang time to say anything, the chief's warrior handed Chang a knife and spear and pointed toward the jungle.

"Go now, and run fast. The warriors will be dispatched on your trail shortly."

Chang, horrified of what might happen if he was captured, sprinted off into the jungle. He remembered how the panther in Louisiana had tracked him down and bit off his left ear. Chang realized that his days might just be coming to an abrupt and unsatisfactory end.

The chief gave Chang plenty of time to get deep into the jungle before he sent his two best warriors after him. The warriors knew the jungle well and how to track their prey. It was easy for them to pick up Chang's trail and follow.

The two warriors found Chang in short order but did not attack. Instead they forced Chang to change directions many times, as they wanted him to go to a specific location. They teased, taunted, and harassed Chang unmercifully for three long, agonizing hours.

Chang ran like a madman and every time he saw one of the natives he screamed. Their painted faces would suddenly materialize out of the jungle foliage and scream at Chang, startling him so much so that he dropped his weapons when he fled. The warriors played their game with him until they finally had him where they wanted, at the sacrificial ceremonial grounds.

Chang realized his hate-filled days had come to an abrupt end. Standing in the center of the ritual grounds were Professor Diego Garcia, the Chief, and six warriors who were joined by the two who had directed Chang. No one spoke. No one made any threats but Chang knew what was going to happen.

Snail, Teri, Eamon, and Christina were together for a late breakfast; Du-Juan and Juliana were at the table next to them. The excitement of the class, the dives, and Chang were the main topics of conversation. They all wondered what had happened to Chang.

"I hope he's gone forever," was the only comment Teri made.

Professor Garcia arrived in time to bid his farewells to the students in the dining facility. He apologized for being late but explained he had just come from an important meeting. He also said that this class was the most exciting he had ever taught.

"You are going home with some great memories. You will relive these memories for the rest of your lives." He never mentioned the attacks nor did he bring up Chang's name.

Epilogue

One Year Later

Another school year passed. Teri and Snail were visiting Redondo Beach for the summer. Carmine and Elaine had just returned from a trip on their new boat, replacing the *Elaine, et al,* which had been destroyed by Chang's men. Teri had completed her undergraduate requirements in pathology and she was eligible to begin her postgraduate degree coursework in forensic pathology. She had graduated with honors and a perfect grade point average of 4.0.

Elaine asked her if she was considering working on a doctorate degree at UCLA once she completed her Masters.

"That all depends on Snail," Teri replied. If he's invited to an NFL tryout and makes a team, I'd go with him and work on completing my degree wherever he's at. Snail and I have discussed this many times, and we both know that having the doctorate degree would help me land a good job. We just don't know where we'll be. Could be here or somewhere else."

"Regardless of where we are," Snail added, "Teri will get her doctorate degree. I like the idea of being married to a doctor. Sounds really romantic to me."

Snail had enjoyed an exceptional year in football. He had earned NCAA second team All-American honors by leading the Pacific-12 in receiving yards, yards after catch, and in touchdowns with 17. He had also grown another inch in height and gained another twenty-five pounds. UCLA that year earned a Sugar Bowl invitation against Michigan on January 1st in the New Orleans Superdome. He had an exceptional game on the big stage, scoring two touchdowns and gaining 172 yards after catch. UCLA went on to win 21-17 in a very hard-fought game. It turned out to be one of the best Sugar Bowl games played in years.

"Teri, I forgot to tell you," Carmine said suddenly, "but you have a letter from the University in Panama."

He went over to the end table and picked it up. He handed her the envelope. She and Snail sat down at the dinner table. Excitedly she opened it up.

"Oh, look. This is from Professor Garcia." There was also a photograph with the letter. She handed the photo to Snail and began to read the letter aloud:

Dear Teri and Snail,

I just wanted to take a moment and wish you both much happiness and success. Things here at the university have been great but a bit boring since our meeting with Mr. Chang and his men. Thankfully that is all in the past. We must move on.

Speaking of moving on, I have been offered a position at UCLA as a professor in the Ecology Department and the advisor for students traveling to Panama for ecological study. I have not decided if I want to take it as I have so much invested in the youth here in Panama.

You and all the other students in your group were a joy to work with, and I want to wish you all good luck and good fortune in the future. Please stay in touch, as I would like to know what you are doing with your lives.

Take care,
Professor Garcia.

"That was sweet. What's the picture of?" Teri asked as she looked over at Snail. He had a strange look on his face.

Snail looked at his future wife and gave a big sigh. He placed the photograph face up on the table and turned it for her to see it better. It was a picture of a kiosk lined with molas and clothing. The lady manning the kiosk was one of the Darién Indians they met at the farewell dinner. Teri looked at the photo studying it carefully. She asked Snail what was the matter.

"Look at the pole next to the Darién Indian. Do you see it?"

Teri scanned the picture and noticed it. "Yes, I see it."

"Look at it very carefully. What do you see?"

Again she looked closely at the photograph. "Snail, are those shrunken heads hanging on that pole?"

"Yes, they are. Now, look closely at the one at the bottom of the pole. What do you see?"

She studied it very carefully for a few minutes.

"That head is missing part of his left ear. It looks like it was bitten off?" She gasped, looking at Snail. "Snail, do you think that's Chang's head?"

He didn't respond right away but instead took the photograph and studied it again. He nodded without a word.

The two sat in silence for some time.

"I can't say I'm sorry about this," Snail said finally, "and we need to put all this drama with him behind us. Teri, we have each other, and he will never do us any harm again. It's like what Professor Garcia said—it's time to move on."

"You know," Terri said, snuggling into him, "Chang was actually the one responsible for our meeting. That was the only good thing he ever did." She looked at him. "Snail, *aloha au ia oe*."

"Teri Ting Pao Silva, soon to be Teri Ting Pao Silva Cali, I love you too."

The adventure continues in …
The Treasure of Alwilda

Bibliography

Beverton, Terry. *Admiral Sir Henry Morgan, King of the Buccaneers.* Pelican Publications Company, Gretna, 2005.

Edmonds, Carl MD. *Dangerous Marine Creatures.* Best Publishing Company, Flagstaff, AZ, 1995.

Internet Search, GENI, Sir Henry Morgan.

National Geographic Magazine, Vol. 133, No. 2, Feb 1968, Pp 222-257

About the Author

Born in California at the end of World War II, John lived there until his father was transferred to Japan where he graduated from high school. He graduated from Nile C. Kinnick (YO-HI) where he excelled in track and field. He served with the US Army Special Forces for 13 years, then joined the US Department of State and served another 14 years. He has traveled to over 100 countries. He is a graduate of George Mason University with a BS Degree in Education and has a Master's Degree from the University of Leicester, UK. John is married to Joyce and they have 5 children and 8 grandchildren. He and his wife are now retired and living in northern Florida.

www.ingramcontent.com/pod-product-compliance
Lightning Source LLC
Chambersburg PA
CBHW071521100726
47908CB00004B/1249